The fruits of people watching.

Death Included

Edited By Jon Doolan

Chapter One

The last of the evening rays of sun danced off the waters of the calm Aegean Sea, patterns and shimmers coming and going with the movements of the waters. A tapestry of ever-changing art that DCI Davies soaked up while nursing his espresso martini, gently spinning the delicate stem of the glass between his forefinger and thumb, watching the foam topped drink swivel against the cool glass. The three coffee beans, which sat purely for decoration, stayed stock-still, held in place by the foam generated by the cocktail master just ten minutes prior. Davies was amazed that it had taken him to the age of forty-three to have discovered a drink that blended his favourite two beverages – coffee and booze.

There was an argument, he supposed, that drinking espresso so late in the evening would hamper his chances of a restful sleep. Davies wasn't worried. He knew restful sleep was never something he attained anyway.

His thoughts were interrupted by sudden blaring music coming from the makeshift stage. It had been set in front of the three busy bars that lined the rear of the hotel. He guessed a hundred chairs lined the courtyard. He looked

at his watch. It must be time for the evening's entertainment.

The blaring Greek music quickly subsided into a tune he recognised, the DJ giving up his oversized headphones and the live band stepping up to the mike. The Motown theme for the evening was a welcome surprise, to the point where he found himself subconsciously tapping his foot to the opening chords of a Stevie Wonder hit. He had no idea which song it was, and even when the main tune kicked in, he couldn't have told anyone what it was called. Still, he enjoyed the music.

His gaze moved beyond the stage and back out to sea. The ripples in the barely moving water were lit by the bright moon that had deigned to grace the Island from behind the lurking mountain that served as a backdrop to the hotel. A break in the waters caught his eye. Too quick to make anything out, but Davies guessed it was a fish of some kind.

Must have been big.

Briefly, his heart sank at the thought of his children missing all this.

Damn you, Eleanor.

The pain of her leaving still wracked his every fibre. After twenty years of marriage, he had yet to come to terms with her betrayal. Sure, he worked long hours, but he'd always provided for his family and made sure to always bring flowers home at least once a week. She said it was because they'd grown apart, and although she loved him, it just wasn't enough anymore.

Davies wanted to believe her, but his constable, Johns, whom he had do a little digging, had come to another conclusion. There was another man. Of course there was.

He hadn't confronted Eleanor with that... he saw no good coming from it. In his line of work, divorce wasn't anything new. The police force had a damning history of broken marriages.

Perhaps he should have joined team red when he had the chance. None of his old mates who had joined the fire service were divorced. None.

Too late now, you old bastard.

This should have been a holiday for the whole family. A week on the tiny paradise island of Kos. But Eleanor had decided that it was best for her and the kids that none of them went. Instead, she'd buggered off to Florida with Albie and Coral to see her sister. Said that Disney and the parks would be a better tonic for them. He could see her point, but she'd told him so late that he couldn't cancel the trip.

It was actually Eleanors sister that had pushed him to come anyway. Said it would do him the world of good. Begrudgingly, he had to agree. The sunshine was a welcome change, and God knows his greying skin from hours of paperwork in the gloomy police station appreciated it. The all-inclusive nature of the hotel took away any sense of stress, and he idled away the hours catching up on years of missed reading for pleasure. He sighed and took another sip of his cocktail.

Damn, that was good. He'd have to leave a tip next time he went the bar.

There was a sudden commotion across the plaza. Near the smaller of the three bars, beyond the gyrating three-piece band that were churning out another classic.

His instincts drew his focus with laser precision, but the noise dissipated as soon as it had started and whatever it was, it wasn't enough of a scene to bring the band to a halt. Probably just someone dropping a glass, inebriated as many of the hotel guests were after another day of sunshine and beer. He glanced at his Elliot Brown watch. Eleven O'clock. All-inclusive

7

certainly had its drawbacks. Davies pitied the staff that worked ridiculously long hours, serving the thankless guests from all over Europe. Guests that were suffering from a sense of entitlement that was clearly undeserved. Like they'd paid up front to be obnoxious alcoholics for a week, devoid of kindness or gratitude. Sometimes Davies loathed the human race.

Of course, there were exceptions. Those that he had spoken to throughout his four days in the hotel so far had genuinely been polite and interesting. Hell, one even knew all about classic cars and had gotten Davies pondering the purchase of a 'doer-upper' although deep down he knew that was ridiculous. When would he ever have the time to get oil under his fingernails?

He let the dream linger, however. Isn't that what holidays are for? Laying in the sun and dreaming?

Time passed slowly and Davies fought every instinct in his body to just get up and walk away. Perhaps even grab the next flight out. Sitting still and do nothing wasn't for him. But he had promised his sister-in-law that he would at least try.

Taking a long draw from his drink, he contemplated trying a different cocktail to finish the evening before retiring to his room and another restless night. A negroni tickled his fancy. Yes, that's what he'd have.

As if reading his mind, or perhaps his body language, a young girl in the black and white of the hotel uniform stood by his table for one. She held a tray in her right hand, perched up high near her shoulder. She shifted her weight to her left hip, balancing the weight of the empties stacked over the round tray, hand on her hip, elbow out. It was seductive yet practical.

Her name badge read 'Pippa.' A smile spread across his tired face, hoping to replicate the amused look he was receiving.

"Another Martini, sir?" She asked, the friendly smile genuine.

The way her ears lifted as she smiled left a chasm in his heart. She looked so much like his sister, Amelia.

How he missed her.

Feeling oddly under pressure to agree, he replied "Well, just one more then"

"Of course. Same again?"

Davies looked down at his glass as if confused as to what she was asking before sheepishly asking "I think I'll try a negroni please"

Pippa gave a curt nod, the smile never fading. "I'll be right back with your drink. Don't go anywhere!"

Davies watched her walk towards the bar and stop at another table and take an order, never writing anything down. All in the head. With a memory like that, she'd make a fine detective.

What was that all about man?

The striking resemblance to Amelia had shaken him up.

Get a grip.

Shaking his head as if the physical act would rid him of the painful memories, he turned his attention to the couples around him, playing cards and laughing at their little jokes shared. Perhaps they were laughing at the people around *them*. Maybe they were laughing at *him*, sat all alone. He dismissed the thought. Christ, he was doing the same thing. For some reason he kept being drawn to the man with an unfortunate nose. Years of excessive alcohol consumption had made his nose bloated and red. Why wouldn't you get some sort of plastic

10

surgery? Perhaps Rhinoplasty? Isn't that what nose surgery was called? He'd have to google that.

The evening drifted by, as had the previous two in the hotel, and he finished his sour negroni. Not bad, but not an espresso martini. Not at all.

Davies awoke from a fitful sleep at 6.30 a.m. He reluctantly grabbed an instant coffee from his room that would hopefully fuel his morning walk. He briefly studied his image in the mirror, pleased that the sun was easing the bags under his eyes, even bringing a little spark to hazel brown eyes.

Not bad for an old man.

His wore his slightly greying hair an inch or two longer than Eleanor liked; the curls of a misspent youth in Newquay slowly returning. The same years of daily surfing had forged broad shoulders that to this day he was proud of. Daily press ups kept the mid-forties man boobs from appearing, and the twice weekly 10k runs exercised his mental demons as well as keeping the gut under control. At six foot on the nose, he was neither tall nor short.

He enjoyed the early morning and its peaceful air. Only the odd hotel employee was up and working at that time – that he could see anyway. He imagined that behind the scenes they were busying away preparing the day for the guests. A nightmare Groundhog Day full of false smiles and platitudes.

He stepped out of his room and sucked in the fresh, warm air and set off towards the beach. A stiff breeze greeted him as he ventured out from the protection of the hotel building. To his continued amazement, there were some guests already up and about, no doubt scurrying off to reserve their spot for the day with the time-honoured placing of the towel.
Absentmindedly, he wondered if they really were Germans. He chuckled to himself, overhearing the harsh tones of the German language from a couple clutching their pale-green, hotel-issue towels. Some stereotypes really were accurate.

Passing by the rather chilly first of the five pools, he casually walked down the path towards the sea, but something caught his eye. Curious as a detective should be, he stopped and focused his attention on the stark-white thing he'd spotted. Unable to discern what it was, he changed direction and walked a different path, this one taking him towards the half-covered day beds and the fake beach lined pool.

A thousand crime scenes flooded his consciousness. He knew exactly what he was looking at well before he drew close enough to see with any real detail.

He was looking at a body.

Fuck's sake.

He quickened his pace and was 'on scene' within seconds. Half in and half out of the pool laid the body of a woman. Her legs and black skirted backside were gently bobbing in the water. Her upper body lay silent and unmoving on the sand, her left arm stuck awkwardly above her head, her right tucked under her body. The right side of her face was partially covered by her auburn hair, which he brushed aside and touched her neck with two fingers, searching for a pulse. Her skin was cold and despite deep down knowing the truth, he persisted with his attempts at finding signs of life, this time trying for a radial pulse.

Nothing.

Shit.

Still no pulse. He gently lifted her right eyelid.

Nothing.

Oh, Jesus fucking Christ...

The sudden realisation of who the poor woman was hit him like a sledgehammer. He was crouched over Pippa, the girl who had served him the night before. The girl who'd reminded him of his Amelia. A thousand haunting images flooded his consciousness, his limbs grew weak, and his head swam.

"No, no no..." He whispered; his voice distant as if someone else had said the words.

He desperately searched for a pulse again, silently praying to a God he no longer believed in.

Nothing.

Davies resisted flopping down onto the floor, scared he'd compromise the crime scene. Suddenly, he found himself in a quandary. Call for help and make a scene? Or sidle off and get help? No. That risked a child or a family stumbling across the Pippa. That wouldn't do. He couldn't leave her.

Looking around for someone, he spotted a Scottish couple he'd spoken to a few nights previous.

"Ben!" he shouted under his breath, the word coming out hoarse and strained. Neither Ben nor his charming wife saw or heard him, so he tried a little louder, arms waving. "Ben! Over here!"

That got their attention. They both waved back, clearly confused by his overly enthusiastic early morning greeting.

Davies waved them over. "Quickly. Come here. It's urgent!" He tried not to sound desperate, or he supposed, weird.

The couple glanced at each other before backtracking around the sun beds and over the little wooden bridge.

As they approached Davies, he tried to position himself between them and the unfortunate woman.

"Morning, guys" Davies said, awkwardly upbeat. "Sorry to bother you but, er, there's been an... incident here that I've just come across."

Davies was glad that he'd revealed his occupation back home, otherwise they might have reacted differently. For the life of him he couldn't remember the girl's name. What kind of detective was he? Forgetting names?

You need to address that man.

"Oh my god!" The young Scottish lass exclaimed, her hand shooting up to cover her mouth. Her ginger hair was raked back into a single ponytail, revealing a close crop of freckles, the suntan lotion showing in streaks where she hadn't rubbed it in properly. "Who's that?" she asked.

Ben clearly hadn't spotted the corpse yet.

"Is she deed?" the Scottish accent clear as day.

"Dead?" Ben asked, seemingly dragged into the present by the word. A stocky man with biceps that strained the sleeves of his T-shirt and neck as thick as a tree, he exuded power, yet Davies reckoned he'd beat him in any foot race.

Davies shrugged his shoulders "I'm afraid she is. I've just found her. We need to call the police, but I don't have my mobile with me. Can one of you run up to reception and get them to make the call? I don't want to leave the body and let it upset anyone else... more than the whole thing is going to anyway."

Ben quickly snapped into action. "Of course. Yes. I'll go now..." He placed a hand on his wife's shoulder, silently asking if she was okay.

"Go!" she urged, acting a lot more controlled since the initial shock.

They both watched Ben trot off back towards the main building.

"She's definitely deed?" asked the fiery-ginger-haired woman, whose name still escaped him. Her emerald-green eyes sparkled, the guilty excitement of the moment there to see. The unkept eyebrows were both refreshing and surprising as was the dark tattoo on her neck that had been hidden by her hair on previous meetings. What was it? A fairy?

Davies scrunched up his face. "Well, I can't pronounce her as dead, but no, there are no signs of life." He swallowed his rising anger. It wouldn't be fair to take out his anguish on her.

He received a knowing nod, but noticed her hands shook. Excitement and adrenaline do funny things to the body. "Look. We need to protect the scene for evidence and from onlookers. Can you head back up the path and encourage any early risers to go a different way? At least until a member of staff can take over."

"Aye," she replied, now eager to distance herself from death. "But what can I tell them?"

"Tell them there's broken glass over here, and until it's swept up, it's dangerous."

"Aye. No reason to doubt that ah suppose."

"Thank you." Davies said and urged her on her way with a gentle wave of his hand down by his hip. Subtle yet powerful.

She nodded, spun around and set off to do her duty.

Give civvies a specific task and it takes their mind off the horror. Makes them feel important.

Fuck's sake, Antony. This was meant to be a holiday!

Trouble always seemed to find him. This specific trouble laid at his feet and would remain there until someone from the Greek police arrived. The fact that he'd yet to see a single member of the police since he'd been on the island didn't instil much hope that they'd be quick to arrive either. Did they have any detectives on the island? Would it just be a uniformed officer? Davies set himself up for a wait and made a mental note to make sure that when a member of staff arrived, they'd go grab him another coffee. He really needed more caffeine.

Chapter Two

An hour passed. No police. Just him and Pippa.

The hotel duty manager – Funella – had organised some makeshift privacy screens that the hotel staff had arranged around the crime scene as best they could under the supervision of Davies. The last thing he wanted was for the scene to be contaminated beyond what he'd already done. The screens were a combination of beach wind breakers and genuine medical screens that he presumed had come from the small first aid office located at the heart of the hotel.

"Where are the police based?" Davies asked Funella after she'd given yet more instructions to her willing staff.

Funella sighed. "There are some local police in Kardemena, but they are just simple officers, good for drunk tourists and speeding cars. No, the only proper police officer we have is based in Kos town."

"Are they on their way?"

"So I am told... but Detective Konsa isn't, what would you say, eager?"

"I see. Is he good though?" As soon as he asked the question, he knew it was a stupid one. How was she to know if he was any good at his job?

"I do not know Mr Davies. These are things I do not get involved with."

"My apologies. That was a stupid question. I only ask because I am a police officer in the UK..."

"Yes. This I know. This is why I allowed you to stay here."

Davies paused, unsure what Funella's attitude towards him was. She stood tall, her back stiff. The severe look of a school headmistress was only added to by the angular and stern features she kept tight and knitted by the frown she seemed to be permanently fixed with.

"Thank you. In the UK, I'm a detective and have been for nearly 20 years. This is your hotel, and I abide by your rules, but if it is OK with you, I'd like to take some initial notes on the scene." Davies saw the doubt in Funella's eyes so added, "...before the wind picks up and disturbs any evidence. Anything I gather or note, I will of course hand over to Detective Konsa as soon as he arrives."

Funella paused, deep in thought. Davies silently urged her to agree. It would be much easier if she worked with him. He sensed that this Konsa wouldn't be the best man to work the case, and although Davies didn't want to or indeed shouldn't need to get involved, he could at least set the Greek detective on the right path.

Finally, Funella came to a decision. "Very well, Mr Davies. I can see your logic here. Is there anything I or my staff can do to help?"

"Thank you. Okay, do you have any little clear bags? Like the ones you have on an aeroplane for your toiletries?"

Funella considered his question, her bleach blonde graduated bob coming loose from behind her left ear where it had been tucked. A lifetime of doing so had made her ears protrude ever so slightly. Davies liked her with her hair a little more relaxed. Made her seem less severe. In an action practiced a million times, she tucked the rogue lock back and answered his question. "Yes, we have something similar, I think. We have pre-packaged female welfare packs in case, well, I'm sure you understand?"

Davies did. Patrol cars carried such packs these days.

"That would be perfect. Thanks. I'll also need some cotton buds or perhaps the doctor's office has some swabs? Come to think of it, is there a doctor on duty here today?"

"Today is Wednesday?" It was a rhetorical question. "So no, not here, but our sister hotel, the Blue Dominias will have Doctor Karagounis on duty at ten."

Davies glanced at his watch. 7.45. "Can you send...?"

"Her."

"Her, here as soon as she arrives?"

Funella nodded encouragingly. "Yes, of course."

Davies got the feeling that by having Dr Karagounis in attendance, Funella would feel a lot more comfortable.

"Anything else, Mr Davies?"

Davies smiled encouragingly and dug in his pocket for his room key which he held out in offering "Could you send someone to fetch my phone from my room? I'll need to take some pictures."

"Of course," Funella nodded, taking the key.

She was about to turn away when Davies added. "And I don't suppose I could get a cup of coffee, could I?"

Funella nodded again, "Yes, Mr Davies. I'll have one brought down. Milk? Sugar?"

"Thank you. Just a little milk, please." Davies like it strong, but with enough milk to take away the bitterness.

Funella turned sharply and went to deliver her instructions to a waiting junior manager who stood at a parade ground 'at ease'. Funella ran a tight ship it seemed. Good. That would make things easier for Davies in the short term.

While waiting for his phone and coffee, he took in the scene again. The top half of the Pippa body wasn't wet. Only the bottom half that was in the pool. Had the heat of Kos been enough to have dried out her clothes, or had she only been half in the water? He gently slid a hand under her stomach and found her blouse to be wet too. Again, fully submerged and dried or had the water slowly wicked up into her top? The sand on the artificial beach looked consistently the same but under closer scrutiny it was apparent that the area in front of her splayed body had been smoothed over. It was a little neater than the rest of the sand and there were clear sweeping lines where something had been used to possibly cover tracks? Had the body been dragged into this position?

She had sand in her hair, and he noticed that there was sand in her slightly open mouth. He wouldn't touch that until either the doctor or Konsa arrived though.

He couldn't see any bruising or marks on the side of her face that wasn't buried in the sand, neither was there any on her neck. Under closer scrutiny, there appeared to be a small splatter of blood on her white blouse, just under her left breast.

Placing the back of his hand on her neck where he had previously tried to find a pulse, he noted that although still warm, she had cooled considerably. Without massive blood loss being evident, it would suggest that she had been dead for a few hours by this point.

His thoughts were interrupted by a new voice that made him jump "I'd be interested in your thoughts, DCI Davies."

He jumped up and spun round to be greeted with a warm smile by a woman. Tightly curled brown hair, olive skin, intelligent blue eyes. She was clutching a silver samsonite case.

"Hello!" Davies spurted, struck by the woman's beauty.

Her smile widened. "Sorry to make you jump. My name is Dr Karagounis"

Davies heart skipped a beat "Oh hi."*Grow up man! You're still married... just about.*

"Sorry," he apologised "I... I, wasn't expecting you so soon..." He glanced at his watch as if to emphasise the point.

Karagounis placed the case on the floor and offered her hand which Davies gladly took. Her skin was exceptionally smooth, yet she had a firm and confident grip.

"Normally, you are right. I don't begin until ten, but as well as being a doctor for the hotels, I am also the island police pathologist. I received the call about Pippa." Her smile faded a touch. "So sad"

"You knew her?"

Of course she knew her, idiot!

"It is a small Island."

"Of course. I'm sorry, Doctor"

"Thank you. Now, if you please, would you update me on the scene?"

"Of course... can I ask how you knew I was DCI?"

The doctor gave a relaxed shrug of her slender shoulders. "The Scottish couple pointed you out, telling me that everything was under control. They were keen to impress your credentials."

Good enough.

"I have I.D if you'd like to see it? It's in my room..."

Karagounis gave a non-committal shrug.

Smiling an understanding, he duly ran through the events of the morning and gave her his thoughts so far.

Karagounis nodded and grimaced as he did so. "Excellent. Nice to have such a thorough brief..."

Surprised at her honesty, he asked, "So, the Island Detective... you're not impressed?"

She suddenly looked embarrassed. "My apologies. That wasn't very professional of me, was it?"

Davies gave her an understanding smile. He'd come across many incompetent people through his years in the Thames Valley Police Force and felt her frustrations.

"Anyway, now that you're here, it's your crime scene until Konsa arrives. I'll take a back seat and let you do your job. If you need me, I'll be stood back enjoying my... Ah! My coffee!"

A hotel employee that he recognised as Mario hurried down the path and handed Davies his coffee and phone.

"Thank you, Mario," Davies said beaming. He really did love his coffee.

"No problem, sir. Double espresso with a little milk"

"You know me so well!"

Mario gave one of his infectious grins. Of all the staff at the hotel, Mario undoubtedly had the most energy and Davies liked him for it.

His smile quickly faded when he saw Pippa though.

Davies couldn't help himself. "You work the same bar as Pippa, don't you?"

Mario sighed. "Yes. Yes, I did. This is just fucking terrible." Realising what he'd said, added, "My apologies for my language."

Davies waved it away "Were you working last night?"

"I was." Mario started biting a nail on his right hand. Davies could see that all of them were chewed down to the quick.

"Pippa too?"

Mario nodded and looked solemnly at the corpse. Davies glanced to see that Karagounis had her case open and had started her examination.

Turning back to Mario, Davies continued. "And how was Pippa? Did she seem ok? Did anything happen that seemed unusual last night?"

Mario suddenly looked uncomfortable. Embarrassed even. "Well, it is not unusual for Pippa to be, how you say, grumpy? She wasn't happy last night, especially after the incident..."

Davies interested was piqued, as was Karagounis who'd stood and joined them.

She seemed okay when she served me. "Go on" Davies urged.

Mario looked at the doctor as if for support. Karagounis nodded her encouragement.

Mario sighed. "There was a hotel guest being very awkward, and Pippa didn't take it too well. She started arguing with him and he shouted back. They were causing a scene, so I tried to stand between them and calm Pippa down before she got into real trouble..."

"And then?"

"Then, well... she slapped me."

Karagounis glanced up in surprise.

"She slapped you?" Davies asked, noting the Doctors reaction.

"It's okay. She calmed down once others had moved her out the back. We gave the guest what he wanted, and by the time I went to see her, she was very sorry and apologised a lot. It's ok. We work long hours and sometimes we get angry. It's okay."

"What time was this?"

"About 11p.m."

Davies remembered the commotion.

"And when was the last time you saw her?"

"Just after two when we closed the bar. She had been sent to a different bar to see out her shift, but then she came back to help me clean. She is... she was, a good worker."

"And she was okay by then?"

Mario shrugged. "As good as she was going to be."

Davies mulled the information over before placing a reassuring hand on his man's shoulder.

"Mario, I'm going to need you to tell all of that to the detective when he arrives, okay?"

"Sure thing, boss. If you don't need me until then, I have work to do."

"Of course. Don't go too far though, eh."

Mario dragged up one of smiles. "I'll be at the bar, boss. Oh! I forget, I also have your phone!"

He handed over the large smartphone before turning back the way he'd come and disappeared out of sight.

Karagounis spoke first. "That doesn't sound good."

"No, it doesn't. It'll be up to Detective Konsa to follow that up and find out who the guest was."

Karagounis grimaced, and Davies gave her a knowing smile. "Tell me what you see, Doctor," he said, keen to get her thoughts on the scene before Konsa arrived.

Crouching back down, she pulled on some new blood gloves. She handed Davies a pair before taking out her large digital camera. She began taking photos of the scene and then the body, talking as she worked.

"Initial information puts the victim's death somewhere between two a.m. and, what would you say? Six thirty?"

Davies nodded. "Yes, I was down here just after six thirty."

"That matches my initial TOD based on body temperature and skin colour." She leant down to inspect Pippa's face and snapped a couple of close-up shots. "There appears to be sand in and around the mouth, suggesting possible choking or asphyxiation. An autopsy would be required to see if there is any sand or other foreign objects in her throat, lungs or stomach."

Davies watched, quietly impressed as the doctor went about her business.

Karagounis continued. "There is no evidence of any bruising or contusions in or around the face and neck and no signs of any blood... hang on, no, there is a small amount of congealed blood and sand that appears to be coming from the victim's right nostril...and yes, there is blood on her blouse."

"Good spot," Davies added, needlessly.

Karagounis gave him a brief yet withering look. Suddenly she didn't look quite so beautiful.

"In the surrounding area there is signs that the sand has been disturbed in a way that suggests it has been moved to cover footprints, but that would need confirming with the ground staff..."

Davies indicated that he'd made a note to do just that and Karagounis continued. "The lower half of the body is in the pool water and the upper is on the artificial beach. The clothing on the upper half appears to be dry, suggesting that it had never been in the water."

"Sorry to interject, Doctor, but if this had been in the early hours, would the climate here have been sufficient to have dried out her clothing if it had indeed been in the water?"

Karagounis blushed "Yes, of course. Forgive me."

"No problem. I expect you work long hours also?"

"That's no excuse, but…" she clearly wanted to redeem herself, "If she had been fully submerged, then the clothing that is face down in the sand will still be wet or at least damp. Also, the blood on the blouse… if she had been in the water, that blood would have spread on the material."

Davies gave her what he hoped was a rewarding smile. He sensed that he would need to keep her on board.

"We need to wait for Detective Konsa to arrive before we move the body," she said.

"Agreed."

Karagounis did a quick 360 of the scene before asking, "Have you seen her shoes?"

Of course! Idiot. Davies chided himself for not noticing himself.

"No…"

Pathetic.

Karagounis seemed to regain some confidence from having noticed something he hadn't.

Davies cleared his throat. "That would be an odd memento to keep."

"Agreed, but not unheard of, no?"

Davies thought back to dozens of cases he'd worked on. "Murderers – if that is what this is – have been known to keep any number of strange things."

"Murder?! That is something I will decide!" A gravelly male voice. Flustered, annoyed and with a thick Greek accent.

Davies ignored the voice and looked at Karagounis, judging her reaction. She grimaced as she stood and fixed a strained smile on her face, ready to welcome the newcomer.

"Who are you and why are you here?" The voice was now much closer. Still Davies didn't react, instead sipping at his coffee. "Doctor! Who is this in my crime scene!" The voice had gone up an octave and Davies imagined the owner's face turning crimson.

Davies held up a hand to gently silence the doctor and instead turned to face the newcomer. "Detective Konsa, I assume?" He thrust out his hand and fixed the man a smile.

Cool it, Davies.

He needed to reign in the attitude. Seeing Pippa laying there had gotten to him. The general attitude towards Konsa hadn't helped.

Form your opinion. That's what he told the young officers coming through the service.

Konsa ignored the proffered hand. If they'd been in a cartoon, steam would have been pouring from his ears such was his obvious anger. "And who are you?!"

Davies kept his hand out in a peace offering. "Davies. I discovered the body this morning."

Konsa still refused to take his hand, but he softened a little. "Well," he huffed. "That is good. I will need to take a statement, but you are going to ruin my scene. If you would kindly step away."

"Of course. I need a top up of my coffee. I'll be at the bar. Can I get either of you something?"

Konsa ignored him and Karagounis began to defend him "But he is a..."

"It's okay. I know when I'm in the way. You guys have a job to do." And with that, he slowly made his way back up to the hotel. Although every professional fibre in his body wanted to stay and work through the scene. He was also keenly aware that if the roles were reversed, he'd be just as angry as Konsa was right now. Besides, he had no real evidence to say that Konsa was in fact inept.

As he walked, he could just hear Konsa having a go at the poor doctor and her desperate attempts to defend her decision to let Davies stay. "But he secured the scene..." was the last he heard.

Not your problem, Davies.

With that he ordered another coffee from Mario and helped himself to some morning baklava.

Chapter Three

Davies had finished his coffee and had grown tired of waiting for a possible reappearance of Konsa, seeking his help, so decided to go back to his room before heading down to the beach. He didn't get far before a member of the hotel staff came to him and asked if he'd come with them. It seemed Detective Konsa had requested him. The young woman led him back to the crime scene by the pool.

"Thank you," Davies said, already assessing the scene once again. Konsa and or Karagounis had pulled the body from the pool and Pippa now laid on her back on a sun lounger. He wasn't sure why they'd lifted her onto that and for some reason it just made the whole thing look wholly wrong in his eyes. A dead body on a sun lounger?

Konsa broke off his conversation with Karagounis and greeted Davies with a little more warmth, this time proffering his hand "My apologies for earlier, DCI Davies. I was unaware of your, er job. Perhaps if you had told me at the beginning...?" He let the question hang before adding. "It would seem though that I have you to thank for preserving the crime scene and setting things in motion."

Davies took the offered hand but merely shrugged off the thanks and ignored the question.

Karagounis, for her part, busied herself by taking more photos of the scene. Every FSI he ever worked with took an unholy number of pictures.

Konsa looked uncomfortable. Perhaps he was unaccustomed to apologies? At least offering them anyway. "I have officers at the main doors, so I'm afraid that if you need to leave the hotel, that won't be possible."

"I have nowhere to go," Davies replied. "What about the beach? Can people go up and down that? Hard to lock down a hotel. Surely there's people due to leave today? More to arrive?"

"Of course, and we have identified those people, and they will be the first to be interviewed. As for the beach... you make a good point DCI Davies. My problem is manpower. I am awaiting more people to arrive from Crete as backup, but until that time I am the only detective on the island..."

"That's not going to make things easy or quick" Davies pointed out.

"When is an investigation ever quick?"

"It needs to be in the early part. Things have a habit of going missing, being covered up or in this case, just plain leaving."

"Point taken."

"Can I ask a question?"

Konsa shrugged noncommittally.

"Do you think the person or persons we are seeking is someone from the hotel?"

"It is highly likely. Security at the resort's gate wouldn't allow anyone who's not a guest or staff to enter."

"And they keep logs of those who do?" Davies wanted to know.

Konsa looked uncomfortable again. "I am certain they do not"

"Contractors? Deliveries?"

"I'm sure the hotel must keep a log of that, yes. I will ask..."

"Funella?"

"Yes, Funella, the manager. Thank you, DCI Davies,"

"No problem. Any sign of her shoes?"

Konsa looked at the doctor, clearly unaware of the shoe question.

Karagounis said, "Not so far, but we haven't gone any further than this scene yet."

Konsa looked annoyed but kept it in check.

"DCI Davies, it pains me to tell you that I have been ordered, from HQ, to ask for your assistance. That is until officers arrive from Crete you understand?"

Well, that's a turn up for the books...

"Has the question been asked of my boss?"

Konsa clearly did not want this. Unless of course grinding your teeth in Greece was seen as act of joy. "No. Do you have the number for your boss?"

"I do. She'll probably tell you that I need a holiday, but there's only so much reading I can do. If she agrees, then I will help where I can. I do not wish to step on your toes though, detective..."

Konsa seemed to appreciate the acknowledgement of the awkward situation.

"Very well, DCI Davies. We have a lot of people to interview..."

"Perhaps we start with the people involved in the altercation?"

"Altercation?"

"Apologies, detective. I asked some questions this morning. It seems there was a small incident last night."

Davies outlined what he had been told by Mario all the while studying Konsa.

"Very interesting. We shall talk to this Mario and any staff that were working that area. We must also locate the guest and any witnesses. I will split the team blocking the main entrance. One of them can organise this."

"Good idea."

Konsa now addressed Karagounis. "Doctor, is there anything else you need?"

"I will need help to get the body onto a stretcher when the ambulance arrives. Until then I am finished here."

"Very good. You can perform the autopsy as soon as you get to the hospital?"

"Of course."

"Good." Now addressing Davies, "I will go call your boss and organise somewhere for interviews."

With that, Konsa strode off towards the hotel, self-importance emanating from every pompous movement.

Davies thrust his hands into the pockets of his shorts and looked a little sheepish. "Well," he began "He doesn't seem too bad..."

Karagounis laughed "That well may be the case, but let us just see, shall we?"

Davies changed the subject. "Your English really is superb, Doctor. Did you study it in school?"

It was the doctor's turn to look sheepish, "Thank you. I studied medicine in London. It was a very much a case of being thrown in at the deep end when it comes to learning a language properly. Some say the best way."

Noting the cute way she tucked a rogue lock of hair behind her ear he said, "Well, I'm impressed."

An awkward silence followed which Karagounis broke first. "Would you be able to help with the body when the ambulance arrives?"

"Of course. If Konsa gets my boss's approval to assist, would it be okay for me to join you in the autopsy?"

Karagounis looked surprised, if a little pleased. "I cannot see the Konsa allowing this. It would, however, make a nice change to have a detective take an interest."

Cutting.

"Also, you should know that the blouse was damp as opposed to being wet. It is my opinion that this is from the wet sand and not from being submerged."

"Good work, Doctor."

Before he could finish, she added more "And Konsa spoke to a groundsman. The way the sand had been moved... it wasn't in a way that they do it."

"Excellent. That reinforces what you noted earlier. In the meantime, I think I will take a little time to spread my search for the missing shoes. Shouldn't be too hard to spot amongst the flip flops and beach shoes if they are around."

"Where will you start?"

"I guess I'll trace routes back to the hotel from here, then check to see If there is a staff room of sorts and then make my way down to the beach." As an afterthought added "I assume Pippa had digs here at the hotel?"

"Digs?"

"Sorry, Accommodation? Or was she a local?"

"Ah, I see. No, she was from the mainland I believe, so yes, she will have a room in the staff block."

Davies made a mental note to add that to Konsa's to-do list.

"Excellent. Thank you, Doctor. You have been most helpful."

"As have you been, Inspector."

Another awkward silence fell between them before Davies backed away, smiling goofily.

Was there a spark there?

Davies began his meticulous search of the grounds via the main reception desk where he found Konsa on the phone. He asked where the staff room was, Konsa's nod of approval was enough for the receptionist to comply. Before he could head off with the Albanian porter,

Konsa mouthed that he had been given approval to integrate Davies into his force. Davies gave a curt nod of acknowledgment and followed the Albanian.

The staff room was empty save for a couple of chefs who dozed in the corner on faux leather chairs, their kitchen whites grubby and creased from the breakfast extravaganza. The room was surprisingly tidy and there were no errant pairs of shoes to be seen. Davies thanked the Albanian porter and resumed his search down towards the beach.

The hotel was busy with the morning breakfast rush, which his grumbling stomach reminded him that all he had eaten was some Baklava. It also meant that the beach hadn't begun to fill up yet. The morning had clouded over a bit and so there was also less of a rush for the sun worshippers to claim their spot.

The beach was covered in sunbeds and grass covered parasols that were fixed in place, which incidentally made it difficult to maintain full access to the sun. People would systematically move their beds around as the day went on in an effort to avoid the shade of the parasol. It didn't bother Davies who, if he was to venture to the beach, just wanted to read his book.

There was a small beach bar and two eateries at the beach along with the water sports centre. All breeze block construction with a freshly painted white render. He had planned on doing some dives while here, but his secondment had put paid to that particular idea. He shrugged it off. Sad as it may seem, he was rather pleased that he had found some work to do. Gave him some purpose. Helped to keep his brain from turning to mush. Better than one of those damn sudoku puzzles.

He'd yet to paddle in the sea, so decided to make his way to the water and take in the hotel from a different perspective. Holding his flip flops in his left hand, he found the water was warmer than the pool, but the sandy gravel was uncomfortable on his feet. He quickly began to sink, necessitating constant movement. In the distance three smaller islands sat shrouded in cloud which would burn off as the day went on if the sun decided to show its face again.

Davies turned his back on the ocean and faced the hotel. It had a wonderful backdrop of a mountain... range? How many mountains need there be for it to be classed as a range?

It looked dry and crumbly, but he could just make out a track that looked vaguely navigable, at least as far as the white and blue church that stood proudly along its face. The clean lines of the church were a stark contrast to the rock-strewn mountain.

Davies played the crime scene over and over in his head. Something about it nagged at him. He was convinced that the murder had happened elsewhere. How far away from the eventual resting place, he wasn't sure, but he was betting that wherever Pippa's shoes were, he'd find more clues.

With his free hand in his shorts pocket, his mind wandered, the sun finally breaking out between some clouds and warming his back.

What happened to you Pippa?

The beach had been cleaned and tidied, the loungers all placed back in their neat little rows, suggesting that if her shoes had been here, they'd have been moved.

Lost property?

Giving up the faint hope that there may be some clues down here, Davies got out of the water, the pebble like sand digging into the soles of his feet. Walking like he was on hot coals, he made it to a boardwalk and took a seat on the little veranda that served the pizza hut. A hotel cook was already needing dough ready for the never-ending demand for pizza. Why people didn't want to eat Greek food, he'd never know. Tzatziki? Hummus? Olives, anyone!?

Brushing off the pebbles, his attention was drawn by the cook who was now cursing and gesticulating at his wood fired pizza oven. Intrigued, Davies raised his head to see what all the fuss was about. Perhaps nobody had restocked the wood store.

The man in his freshly pressed chefs' whites was jabbing his finger in the direction of the oven and then thrusting his hands in the air and looking up to the skies as if asking God himself for strength to get him through whatever challenge he currently faced. Frustration was clear in his face and his gesticulations.

Davies slipped on his memory-foam-soled flip-flops and stood.

Oh, the luxury.

Nobody was around to help so Davies took the few paces towards the man and politely asked what was wrong.

Momentarily surprised by either Davies mere presence or the fact that he was asking if everything was OK, the man replied "No! People think it is funny?"

"I'm sorry, but what is funny?" Davies asked, amused.

In response, the man bent down slightly and pointed, with both hands spread wide, to the inside of the pizza oven. Davies, a good five inches taller than the irritated man, had to bend down significantly to peer into the darkness of the unlit oven. He could just make out two shapes stuffed right at the back of the oven. His heart skipped a beat.

Never!

"Please," Davies said, trying to calm the man. "Please can we get them out of there?"

The man harrumphed, clearly annoyed that he had to retrieve the items from his oven. He grabbed the long-handled pizza paddle and expertly slid it into the bowels of the oven.

Remembering that he had his phone, he paused the chef and, making sure the flash was on, he took several photos of the shoes in situ. Satisfied he let the man continue and a little jiggery-pokery, he managed to get the paddle under the offending items.

"Slowly!" Davies warned the man.

Again, the cook didn't seem too impressed by his warning, but continued with his task.

49

As the light of the day crept up and over the paddle, it served to confirm what Davies had thought.

Shoes.

Comfy, black, practical dress shoes.

Davies held up both hands in the universal signal for STOP! The man froze, his eyes wide, the shoes balanced precariously on the end of the long wooden paddle.

"Why?" the man asked. "Are these your shoes?"

Davies half chuckled, amused that these small, black shoes could possibly be his. "Please, place the paddle down carefully on that surface." He pointed towards the main counter.

The man looked utterly disgusted at the very thought. "But that is where I make the pizza! This is no place for shoes!"

Davies understood his apprehension as he would when he told him why he wanted them on the worktop "Sir, this is a police matter. Those shoes are very important to a case that Detective Konsa is investigating."

Shame and realisation flooded the man's face. "You mean," he breathed, suddenly aware of what he was holding, "that these are Pippa's shoes?"

"That's exactly what I think." Then as an afterthought. "I'm sorry, you clearly knew her. We need to preserve the shoes in case there are fingerprints. You are quite literally holding onto evidence..."

The man gingerly lowered the paddle, a slight wobble beginning. Finally the paddle rested on the worktop and he stood straight, easing out his back. Davies clocked his name bade – Miguel. He let out the breath he had been holding. Davies realised he too had been holding his breath, and rather more discreetly let his out in an almost desperate attempt to regain some composure that he'd lost with his outburst.

"Well done, Miguel. Thankyou."

Miguel wiped the beads of sweat from his brow and puffed out his cheeks. "Now?"

"Now we close the pizza parlour. If the shoes were in there, then who knows what other evidence may be here."

Miguel reached under the counter and produced a 'closed' sign that he hung from two metal loops above the counter.

"Thank you, Miguel. Now, can you use that telephone?" He pointed to the ancient, corded push button phone that hung from the wall "And get hold of Konsa and Dr Karagounis please?"

Miguel seemed pleased and empowered to have a task and snapped to it. "Of course, sir."

Five minutes later both Konsa and Karagounis arrived, one cool and calm, the other sweaty and anxious. No prizes for guessing which was which.

Konsa was breathing heavily, sweat beading between his thick eyebrows. "They are definitely the victim's shoes?"

Davies shrugged. "Based on the footwear that I've seen the staff wear, they do appear to be a shoe that would be worn by someone working here. Whether they belonged to Pippa, I'm hoping the doctor will be able to tell us...?"

Karagounis swept a hand through her shiny hair, composing her thoughts.

No doubt about it. She was sexy.

"They appear to be her size – thirty-seven or thirty-eight I would say. There should be some

DNA inside that would confirm... and of course there could be some from the killer."

Davies looked back at the shoes. 37 or 38. What was that? A four or five? "I assume there isn't a Greek tradition or ritual that involves stowing shoes in pizza ovens?"

Miguel, who was still standing guard over the shoes, grimaced.

"No." Konsa glared at Davies. "It's not like smashing plates after every meal like you Brits think we do, if that's what you mean." The sarcasm and spite wasn't lost on Davies.

Unnecessary.

Davies ignored the attitude for now. "If they are Pippa's then we can assume the killer didn't expect Miguel would spot the shoes in the back of the oven."

"And burn the evidence," said Karagounis.

Davies gave a her an encouraging smile. "Exactly."

Konsa's eyes flicked between the two of them with a touch of suspicion. "Very well, Doctor. If you could confirm whether these are the victim's shoes as quickly as possible."

Davies saw a tightness in her jawline. Konsa had obviously hit a nerve. "As a one-person department, I'll do what I can seeing as I also have an autopsy to perform."

"Back-up is on its way from Crete as we speak, *Doctor.*"

Knuckles turning white she said "First, I need to photograph the scene, if you don't mind stepping back gentlemen?"

"Very well Doctor, but if you could hurry..."

If looks could harm, Konsa would now be hospitalised.

Davies tried to bring a little order to proceedings. "I can see several possibilities here. Either Pippa was murdered down here and then dragged to the pool, or she was killed by the pool and then her shoes brought down here."

Konsa displayed some modicum of competence. "If the shoes were brought here, then we can place a high chance that the killer then made their escape down the beach."

Davies nodded. "And if she was killed here and taken to the pool, we either have a very strong killer or more than one. How far is it from here to the pool? Four hundred metres? Five? Uphill.

That's not easy on your own with a dead weight of what, sixty kilos?"

Konsa screwed up his face. "Possible but unlikely."

"Agreed," Davies said. "But we still need to clear this area before we move on."

"Nearly there" Karagounis said, concentrating on dusting the shoes for prints before placing them carefully in a clear evidence bag she'd plucked from her case of tricks.

"We start now?" Konsa asked, making a point of staring at his watch.

"I haven't even begun dusting the scene for prints." Karagounis pointed out.

"Can't you just let us do it?" Konsa replied, looking at his watch again.

Need to be somewhere, Detective?

"If we had completed your training Detective, then yes. But as that didn't happen.... DCI Davies can you use a fingerprint kit?"

"It's been a while, but yes. I can manage that here if you want to take care of the autopsy."

"Thank you."

Konsa spoke up. "Make the ambulance driver help with the lifting."

Karagounis nodded her thanks, picked up her FSI bag along with the shoes and headed off up the slope and out of sight.

Konsa and Davies began their search of the white Stucco hut under the intrigued eyes of Miguel. The front had an arch above the serving window and the main bulk of the structure was domed, giving it an almost igloo like resemblance. On the thick arch the word Pizzeria was painted in green and red italic letters. Either side of the hatch were two waist high unlit lamps dug deep into the sand. The framing around the glass was in need of paint, the salt air having a ball on the metal.

The two men worked meticulously, Konsa starting from the entrance of the three by two hut and Davies at the far end. Most of the building was taken up by the giant wood fired pizza oven, leaving a preparation area and a small amount of storage. The area was clean despite being on the beach. The lack of sand inside the hut was probably due to the slightly heavier beach sand and the prevailing winds blowing out to sea. The place was clean. There was no sign of a struggle, and the laminated wooden surfaces had been wiped down. Miguel confessed to doing it at the beginning of his shift that morning. With clasped hands, he begged forgiveness for destroying the evidence.

Davies waved his apology away as he continued his search.

Konsa stepped out on the beach, dragged a packet of Karelia from the inside pocket of his jacket and struck a match. He took a deep drag and expelled a blue cloud. It was whipped away in moments by the warm sea breeze. "There is nothing here," he said, sucking on the cigarette once again.

"Then what might this be?" Davies asked, allowing an air of superiority to tinge the words.

"What?" Konsa asked, more interested in the bikini clad woman who walked past.

"Print." Davies said, pointing at the work surface.

He'd found it underneath the main worktop, as if someone had gripped the surface, finger wrapping round and under the now clean laminate.

"That's lucky," said Davies as he brushed powder across the fingerprint. "The other way round and it would have been cleaned off."

Miguel nodded vigorously, a look of relief spreading across his anxious face. He hadn't wiped away every trace of evidence after all.

"Anything your end, Detective?" Davies asked, bagging the print.

"No, nothing. We should move on I think."

Something nagged at Davies, but he couldn't place exactly what. "Okay, but perhaps we should keep this area locked down until we're 100% happy we have everything?" Then quickly added, "But it is of course, your scene and your investigation..."

Konsa agreed but didn't look happy about it all.

Chapter Four

Davies joined the other guests and settled down for some lunch as if he was actually on holiday. He'd booked the á la carte restaurant, which had a lovely view out over the sea which was now bathed in sunshine, the light dancing over the gentle waves. It seems that here on the island, the wind rose and fell erratically. *Must be hard to sail round here*, he mused as he tucked into a plate of grilled octopus.

Delicious.

Knowing he had work to do, he begrudgingly turned down the white wine that would have paired beautifully with the fresh dish from the sea, instead opting for a freshly made Lemonade. He owed it to Pippa to keep a clean head and do all he could to find out what happened to her. He owed it to Amelia.

He couldn't fully relax though. With the case he'd found himself thrust onto smashing its way through his grey matter. What had he missed? Who else could be a suspect other than those involved in the incident the night before?

Mario didn't seem likely but remained on his suspect list. The guest who'd had the argument. Possible he supposed, but you'd have to be a seriously unhinged person to murder someone after a plain argument.

Stop it, Davies. How many murders have you been to that stemmed from reasons far more incongruous than that? The guest is definitely a suspect.

What about the blood on her blouse? Who's was it? Her attacker, or was it from earlier in the night?

Wonder how Konsa is doing with the interviews?

The timeline bothered him too. Something about the shoes and the place they found the body. Why take the shoes down there? What did they gain other than having them potentially burned? What was so special about the shoes?

He finished his lunch, leaving a generous tip for the ever-attentive staff, and made his way back to his room to freshen up. There wasn't much he could do until the autopsy came back or the results from the prints found a match.

After a quick shower, he discounted the instant coffee that was provided in the room and headed down to the bar for a proper coffee made with real beans. He found another man who wasn't Mario serving him and presumed he was being interviewed by Konsa. Taking a seat near a wall so he had a view of the whole lobby, he waited.

Before he'd finished his coffee, Mario appeared and took his place behind the bar.

Moments later, a tall solid looking man with a stern face, cropped blonde hair and piercing eyes marched out from a room whose blinds had been drawn. He looked angry and scowled at everyone who dared cross his path.

He marched past Davies and out towards the pool. Davies followed his path and saw him pull up a stool at the pool bar and order a drink. If that was the man who'd upset Pippa, he probably needed the drink to calm down.

Konsa exited the room next and quickly clocked Davies and made his way to his table.

"I sit?" Konsa asked

Davies waved a hand towards the seat opposite. "Be my guest, Detective."

Konsa sat with the grace of a pregnant hippo, the metal patio chair groaning with the weight.

"How did that go?" Davies asked.

Konsa harrumphed "That man – Victor the Russian? He is not a pleasant man."

"But you don't have anything on him?"

"Not yet. He is a bad man, who is angry at his holiday being, how you say... ruined for two times."

"And?"

"And there is um... motive, but I need fingerprints from the doctor."

As if on cue, Konsa's phone jangled from somewhere deep in the folds of his person. The crumpled cotton jacket did nothing to smarten his appearance or hide the excess weight that he carried. He fished the phone from an inside pocket, studying the screen at arm's length as if he needed glasses. "Ah. It is the doctor."

Davies leaned in, indicating he wanted to hear what she had to say and Konsa duly put it on speaker, dialling down the volume so guests couldn't hear what was being said.

Giatros. Echete new?" Konsa said, his accent thick.

Davies gave him a pained look.

Konsa waved an apologetic hand. "I am sorry. I asked the doctor if she had news."

The silence from the other end suggested Karagounis was waiting for the go ahead.

Davies leaned in and spoke quietly. "Doctor, please tell us what you have found."

"Ah, DCI Davies, I'm glad you are here too. I have completed an initial autopsy."

Her voice stirred something deep down in his stomach. A feeling he'd not had in a long time. Butterflies?

"There are no signs of any bruising on the body except on both wrists. There are also no cuts or abrasions on the body... except grazes on the heels of her feet. The contusions have particles that are consistent with the pathways of the hotel."

"Meaning?" Konsa asked

"That's for you to determine, I think. However, as you know there was sand in and around the mouth. I also found sand in the pharynx, oesophagus and a small amount in the stomach."

Davies jumped on it. "So, she was suffocated by the ingestion of sand?"

"Indeed. It would look as though it was forced into her. But the interesting part is that the sand in the pharynx, oesophagus and the stomach doesn't match the grade of sand in the mouth..."

"What? What does that mean? Sand from where?" Konsa demanded.

I know.

"Without a sample for sure, I cannot confirm, but the makeup of the sand appears to be the same as what is found on the beach."

"Are you sure?" Konsa asked

Karagounis sounded frustrated "As I said, Detective – without a sample, I cannot say for sure."

Davies spoke up. "The sand around the pool was very fine, but the sand at the beach is much coarser. Are we saying, Doctor, that the ingested sand was from the beach and that the sand in the mouth was put there later to mislead?"

There was a brief pause before she answered. "In my opinion, yes, but I'm not the detective."

"Noted," Davies said, his tone soft.

"But why?" Konsa asked, frustration lacing his voice.

"Thank you, Doctor." Davies interjected. "If you could concentrate on the prints, I'd be grateful. We also retrieved another print from the worktop of the pizza parlour. Detective, has that been sent to the doctor?"

Konsa nodded and gruffly replied. "I take care of it."

"Again, thank you, Doctor," said Davies.

"You are welcome." The line went dead.

The two men sat back in their chairs. Davies waited for Konsa to speak first. The silent brooding lasted for a minute or so.

"So, the body was moved?" Konsa asked, lighting up another cigarette.

"Agreed," Davies replied, pleased that the detective had at least come to that correct conclusion. "I would say that she was killed at the beach, the shoes placed in the pizza oven and then the bruises on the wrists suggest that she was then dragged by her wrists to the pool where the poolside sand was put in her mouth in an attempt to deceive us."

"But the killer must be stupid if they think we would not know the difference."

"Possibly stupid. Or maybe it was just a delaying tactic to give them more time to escape."

"From the island?"

"Possible, yes."

"I cannot close the airports," Konsa scoffed.

"No, but if the prints come up with a match, perhaps we'll be quick enough to apprehend them."

Konsa sat deep in thought. Or at least he looked deep in thought.

"I will take the print you found to the Doctor. Get it done."

Misleading. He'd implied that he'd already done that.

"Good idea." Davies put it down to a translation issue.

"You will be ok here?"

"Absolutely, detective."

Konsa stood, with effort, stubbed out his cigarette and left without another word.

Good. Now, I can do my job.

Something still nagged at the back of Davies' brain, but he left it there, stewing. He had other things to check. Starting with the Russian guest.

Victor was still sat at the pool bar. Davies didn't want to question him there, although he was going to keep it as informal as possible.

Here goes.

Davies sauntered over to the pool bar and took the stool two away from Victor. He grabbed a cocktail menu from the bar top and glared at it. Acting annoyed, he turned his attention to Victor, putting the menu down in apparent frustration.

"Excuse me?" Davies said, catching Victor's eye.

"Yes?" The Russian said, his accent thick.

"Sorry, but what is it you are drinking?"

Victor looked confused, looking down at his drink as if only just realising that it was there.

Davies continued. "Your drink. What is it? I can't see anything on the menu like it...?"

Realisation dawned on the strongly built man. "Ah! This drink? It is not on the menu. It is a... special order."

Davies acted intrigued, "Excellent. What is it, please?"

In an overly grand manner as if introducing the latest smart phone that could also drive your car he said, "This is expresso martini!"

Espresso, idiot.

"Oh wow! That sounds amazing! I do love coffee..." Davies feigned intrigue.

"And I love vodka!" Victor laughed heartily.

Davies smiled and continued the charm offensive. "I doubt it is the same as a proper Russian vodka, though. Am I right?"

Victor turned serious and leant in to speak quietly "You speak the truth. No wodka is proper wodka if it is not made in Russia!"

"Is that true? Like champagne? Only champagne if it is made in the Champagne region?"

Victor dialled back the pride but nodded nonetheless. "This is true. wodka is only wodka if made in the motherland."

Jeez. Well, that's a lie. Good. He must think I was born yesterday.

"You learn something every day. Thank you." He signalled the attention of the barman and ordered an espresso martini.

This was one of the less onerous tasks of an investigation he'd ever done. He thanked the barman and took a sip under the watchful eye of Victor.

No doubt about it; that's a good martini.

"Wow!" Davies exclaimed, carefully putting the glass back down "That's my new drink! Thanks..." Davies offered his hand.

"Victor." The big man's grip was strong. Davies' fingers ached but he refused to show it.

"Victor. Any other suggestions?"

"White Russian."

Davies laughed nervously.

"It has wodka, cream and coffee liqueur."

"Oh! It's a drink?" Davies exclaimed, genuinely surprised

Victor looked confused. "Yes. It is drink. What you think it was?"

"Ha! I thought it was some kind of reference to, er, Russian supremacy."

"Ahhh, I see. You are right!" Victor laughed heartily.

Davies took another sip of the delicious cocktail and grinned at Victor. "I had a cocktail up at the other bar yesterday. It was very bad and the woman making it... wow. She was very miserable."

Victor turned serious.

Too soon?

Victor's eyes flicked over to the other bar that was in the distance. "She very angry lady."

Phew. Doubt he'd have said that without the alcohol in his system.

"She is, isn't she?" Davies said, "Haven't seen her today though..."

Victor stayed quiet. Davies didn't feel the need to interject.

The silence hung until Victor buckled. "The police say she is dead."

Davies acted shocked "What! Dead?"

Victor nodded solemnly. "It is true, I think. But they think I did it!"

Davies was properly having to ham it up now. "You're kidding? Why would they think that? That's crazy!"

Now Victor managed to look sheepish. "When she was angry, I say things that she not happy with. But then a waiter try to help and she slap him! It crazy! I feel bad. Maybe last thing she do was shouting at me and slap the man!"

"Wow! What a crazy situation. Is that what the police are doing here?"

"Yes. They interview me. Ask me questions. But I not do these things. After shouting I was... how you say? Sorry? Shy?"

"Embarrassed?"

"Yes! Embarrassed! So wife and me go to beach bar. After that we go back to room. This is holiday. I not want to argue."

Seems genuine.

"Were the police happy with that?"

Victor snorted. "Policeman Konsa. He not good policeman. Ask bad questions. But I have witnesses, and I prove I on computer meeting in night to work."

Davies believed in trusting his gut and right now it was telling him that Victor was innocent. No real proof of that, but if his alibi was legitimate, then that seemed to mostly rule him out.

"Victor, this is a crazy story to tell when you get back home."

"Victor not want story. He just want holiday!"

Davies had heard enough and put on his most understanding face. "I hear you, Victor. That is why we are here, right? Get away from stress?"

"Yes. Work very hard. Victor need holiday."

"Me too, but I need to go and log on and join a work meeting now too. Thanks for the cocktail tip." He raised his glass, downed the drink, smiled, and made his goodbyes.

Sorry pippa. Hope the espresso hits me more than the vodka!

Victor raised his glass, drank and ordered another.

Davies headed for reception. His next stop was Pippa's quarters.

Chapter Five

Securing the key to Pippa's room had proven impossible, so Davies resorted to the old ways. He uncurled the two paper clips he had removed from his hotel welcome pack and slid them into the lock.

Thirty seconds. Not bad.

Again, something nagged at him. A cursory knock before pushing the door open was met with silence, so he pushed his way into the first floor flat.

The block was made up of two floors and sported the same whitewash exterior walls as the main hotel. The wooden features, painted blue and very much in keeping with the traditional Greek vibe, looked a tad more tired than the main hotel, but everything was clean. He'd seen worse staff quarters.

A small tight corridor greeted him as well as the overwhelming smell of gas.

Shit.

He stepped back over the threshold onto the open corridor and shouted. "Hello!? Is anyone there?"

Silence.

Davies sniffed the air. Butane? Propane?

He tried again "Hello? Anyone?"

Again, silence.

Shit. No phone. Idiot. Must have left it in his room again.

Only one thing for it.

Davies took a lungful of sticky Greek air, hoping it wouldn't be his last and entered the flat.

Door to the right. Bathroom. Empty.

Two paces. Door to the left. Bedroom. Cluttered. Empty.

Opposite. Door. Closed. Locked. Three two one. Kick.

The Door flew in.

Bedroom.

Body.

Davies rushed into the room, clocking a pile of portable gas BBQ cylinders. Bending down, he found a young woman.

Pale. Eyes shut. Chest not moving. Get her out.

Davies reached under her arms and went to lift her. Something snagged. What's that?

Her left wrist was handcuffed to the bed which in turn was bolted to the floor. Bending at the knees, he grabbed the base of the metal framed bed and heaved, his lungs screaming. The bed moved a little, but not enough.

Shit. Get the window open.

Davies lunged towards the window, lungs now on fire. Grabbing the handle he twisted, and the window swung open wide into the warm air. Davies stuck his head out and sucked in the fresh air.

Thank God.

Turning back to the scene before him he made a hastily put together plan. He needed a lever. Taking another deep breath of air, he then rushed past the poor girl and back into the corridor, turned right and headed for the door at the end of the corridor.

Closed. Touch the door with the back of his hand. No heat. Twist the Handle. It opened.

Before him was an empty kitchen/living room with a balcony at the far end. Davies quickly scanned the room, searching for something, anything, he could use. Tucked into the corner of the room was a metal pole around a metre in length. Davies rushed over and grabbed it. There was a T shape to one end of it which rotated when he turned the handle at the other. It looked like one of those long handles you use to extend an awning.

Must be one on the balcony.

It felt a little soft. He hoped it wasn't aluminium.

Dashing back into the bedroom, he found the woman unmoved. He slid the bar under the bed frame, braced and heaved. The bed frame creaked in apparent annoyance. Davies ignored the pull of the window and fresh air and heaved one more time. He could feel movement. Then the plug holding the screw into the concrete floor ripped free and the bed frame lifted an inch.

Yes!

Davies dropped the bed, shuffled along so he could reach the handcuff, lifted the bed again and kicked at the cuffs. They cleared the inch square foot of the metal frame.

She was free.

Davies dropped the bed, positioned himself over the woman's head, scooped her up from under arms, stood to a stoop and dragged her out of the room, down the short and narrow corridor and out onto the balcony corridor and more importantly, fresh air. He bumped her down the short set of steps and out onto the tarmac.

I'm so sorry.

He shouted as he went. "Help! Someone help!"

To his surprise, almost immediately someone came out of the flat two doors down. A young good-looking male dressed only in shorts, showing off a tattooed and bronzed chest. His eyes bulged as his mouth began to form a word which never created.

"Ambulance," Davies said slowly, clearly and loudly.

The man nodded and produced a phone from his shorts' pocket and dialled.

Davies turned his attention back to the woman. He hovered his ear over her mouth. Nothing. Her chest neither rose nor fell. Her skin was cool but not cold and he couldn't find a pulse.

Dammit.

Davies used two fingers to lift her chin, then pinched her nose and gave her two rescue breaths. Her cheeks then her chest expanded as his emptied. Then he began the hard work. Interlacing his fingers, right hand over the top of left, he placed the heel of the left on her chest and began compressions. It took four compressions to find the right pressure. He knew because he felt and heard her ribs crack. Inwardly he grimaced. Such a horrible feeling. After 30 compressions he repeated the two rescue breaths, then back to the compressions.

And so it went on. Sweat poured off him, running into his eyes which he tried to blink away, unwilling to stop what he had begun. He knew from experience that time took on a form of its own during these moments. To him it would feel like hours of exhausting work, but in reality, he knew it would be much shorter.

So wrapped up in his work, he'd forgotten about the man in the shorts. He looked up as he resumed another round of compressions, silently playing the Bee Gees song 'Staying Alive' in his head to keep the correct pace. The man was off the phone and staring at Davies. The colour had drained from his face.

"Ambulance?" Davies asked, himself now breathless.

The man just stared at him.

Shock.

"Hey! Ambulance?" Davies shouted a little louder in an effort to shake the man from his stupor. "Is it coming?"

The man blinked violently, clearing the fuzz and recognising what Davies was doing. "Zoe?"

"Is that her name? Zoe?"

"Yes. Yes, it is Zoe. Is she... ok?" Luckily almost everyone in the resort spoke excellent English.

Davies ignored the question, gave two more rescue breaths and resumed the compressions, feeling another rib cracking under his efforts. "How old is she?"

"Twenty-nine."

Looks younger than that even in this state.

"How long till the ambulance arrives?" Davies panted.

"Very soon they say. One is not far away."

Thank God.

"Good. If I get tired, can you take over?" He used his head to gesture down at what he was doing to reinforce what he meant.

Panic struck the face of the man. "No, no. I cannot do that... I am sorry..."

Brilliant.

"Okay. In that case find me a defibrillator"

"A-a what?"

"A machine to jump start her heart."

"Yes! I know!" He immediately span around and set off in his search.

Davies didn't really think a defib was relevant but wanted to give the man a task and it was better to have it than not. What she really needed was oxygen. A lot of it too.

To his amazement he heard the sirens of what he hoped was the ambulance approaching moments before the man returned with the defibrillator.

Rarely had he been so happy to see blue flashing lights. He was just starting another round of compressions when the white and blue ambulance rounded the corner and came to a halt five metres from where Davies sweated and pummelled the poor girl.

Thank God.

Two paramedics disembarked the dust-covered ambulance. The male, mid-forties and the woman who had a timeless look to her didn't need to speak. They'd clearly been a team for some time. The woman – who'd been driving – headed straight for Davies while the man collected their first strike kit from the side door he'd just slid open. The woman made eye contact, smiled grimly and bent down next to Davies. He gave his next two breaths before resuming his compressions for what seemed like the 100th time. He wasn't going to just stop because the professionals had arrived. He would do whatever they needed him to do. He spoke first.

"English?"

"Yes," she said, her velvety Greek voice instantly soothing the situation.

"This is Zoe. 29 years old. Unresponsive. No signs of life. She was in a room full of butane and propane. No idea for how long."

The paramedic nodded her understanding and called something in Greek to her partner who had joined them and was unzipping the bag of tricks.

Davies, for his part, was now tiring with both the effort and the knowledge that he could soon stop what he was doing. Time passed in a hazy dream. He didn't even remember giving up his position over Zoe to the male paramedic.

When did that happen?

In a daze he watched them work. She had a mask over her face. Oxygen? Another man arrived. No shirt. Ah, the onlooker. He needed to speak to him...

Just a moment. Need to catch my breath.

Either he'd been doing CPR for an age, he was getting old, or the heat had whacked him.

Davies shrugged the fug from his head and dragged himself to his feet in time to see the two paramedics load Zoe onto a stretcher.

"I must have blacked out," Davies said, hoping that he was addressing the medical team.

"Are you okay?" The female asked, holding onto the stretcher while the tail lift rose.

"Yes. tired. But okay. Zoe?"

"We'll take care of her."

"Where are you taking her?"

"The hospital is in Kos main town. That's her best chance. We have enough oxygen for her to get there." She closed the rear doors of the ambulance. "You did well there...?"

"Davies."

"...Mr Davies." a kind smile spread across her face. "You are staying here at the hotel?"

"Yes," he said, trying to force some strength into his words.

"Ask the reception to call the hospital later. Hopefully, we can give you news. Do you know Zoe?"

"No. Never met her before. This man does though..." The topless man was stood clutching a defibrillator to his chest. He looked like Davies felt.

The paramedic shrugged. "He's in shock. The police will be here soon. Can you wait for them with this man?" she asked, pointing at topless.

"Of course. Please. We will be ok. Go"

The paramedic produced another warm smile and climbed back into the driver's seat.

The male must be in the back.

Blue lights flashing, the ambulance drove off, a dust cloud in its wake, forcing Davies and the topless man to cover their faces.

When did I get to the ground floor again?

When the dust settled Davies had regained what little composure he could muster and turned his efforts towards the topless man. He had a tattoo of an angel with detailed wings down his right side that ended just above his waistband. Straight black hair was pulled back into a tight ponytail, the sides cropped closed to his head. A light dusting of stubble adorned his angular jaw but the rest of his honed body appeared to be completely hairless.

You're forgetting something, old man.

"Shit" Davies muttered, annoyed at himself. "Sir," he said, his voice assertive, cutting through the shock. "Sir," he said again, moving closer and waving a hand in front of his face. "What is your name?"

"Um. Balague."

"Are you Spanish?"

"Span... oh, my mother is. Was."

"I'm sorry. Balague, can I use your phone? We need the fire service here."

Without a word, Balague thrust his phone out to Davies who took it gratefully and dialled the emergency services. The call was answered immediately, and Davies explained the situation. Clear and to the point. They gave him a reference number which he memorised and promised that a pump would be in attendance within ten minutes.

That done, and while he waited for Konsa and the fire service, he addressed Balague again.

"Son, listen to me. Do you know Zoe?"

Balague looked at him without registering anything, his eyes staring off into the distance.

Give him time. These things can be traumatic, remember?

"Balague," He tried again, placing a hand gently on his shoulder. The human touch seemed to stir him from his stupor once again.

"Sorry?"

Taking his hand off the man's bare shoulder he said, "Son, my name is Detective Davies. I am a police officer from England. I need to ask you some questions, if that's ok?"

"England?"

"Yes. I am working a case here on the island. That led me here to this flat. Now, again, do you know Zoe?"

"Yes. But not very well."

"Why was she in Pippa's flat?"

Balague looked confused "How do you know it's Pippa's flat? Where is Pippa?"

Shit. Either he doesn't know or he's playing me.

"You haven't heard?"

"Heard what?"

Davies didn't want him to go back into another daydream but couldn't lie to him. "I'm afraid Pippa is dead."

There wasn't a scream, a howl or any words. He just looked dumbstruck. Tears began to flow. "W-when?"

"Last night. I am sorry. You knew Pippa as well?"

To Balague's credit, he held it together. "We have worked here for four years in a row. For the last two, we have lived next to each other... How did she die?"

Davies shook his head gently. "I'm sorry, but I cannot say at the moment. Who was Zoe?"

"Zoe? Ah, sorry, yes, she is... was... Pippa's partner."

"To clarify, you mean her lover?"

"Of course."

"Okay, that explains her being there. Have you seen anyone else go into the flat? Anyone else on this balcony?" he asked, pointing up.

"No. Nobody, but I have been working or sleeping. Anyone could have come down here."

"Do Zoe or Pippa have any enemies?"

"Enemies? Of course not!"

"Okay, sorry, I had to ask." Davies held up a placating hand. "Pippa was in a bad mood last night. Do you know why?"

Balague shook his head. "No. Sorry. Pippa didn't talk much and when she did, it wasn't about personal things. Maybe she would have told Zoe... Oh, God. Is she going to be okay?"

"I don't know. The doctors will do their best, I am sure."

This isn't really helping.

"Ok, that will do for now. Why don't you give me that defib and go grab a top? Detective Konsa will want to speak to you when he arrives. Okay?"

Balague gratefully handed over the defib and shuffled up the stairs and back towards his apartment.

Once out of view, Davies slumped down onto the well-tended grass and waited for Konsa and the fire service. They could go in under air and turn off all the gas canisters, although he doubted any had gas left in them. Once done, they could pump the flat full of positive pressure air from one of those giant fans they carry and clear the flat. When they'd done that, he could finally go in and take a look.

Chapter Six

The fire service came out of the property holding their gas monitor and declared the air to be clear. They had left the cylinders in situ, and as expected, they were all empty. Davies, along with the late arriving Konsa, didn't want them to smear their extra-large, filthy fire gloves all over potential prints if they didn't need to.

Having been given the all-clear, they donned shoe covers and entered the flat. Davies talked Konsa through what he had seen and what he had done, which to his surprise was greeted with admiration?

Hell, it was pretty heroic.

They stood at the doorway to the room where Davies had found Zoe, bouncing theories off each other.

Konsa spoke first. "You say that they were lovers? Lesbians?"

"Lovers, yes. Lesbians? I don't know. These days there are so many classifications for sexual, or non-sexual orientations, I wouldn't want to say."

"True. Do you think that this is linked to the murder?"

Davies did well not to snort and strained to keep the derision from his voice "I think it would be highly unusual if they weren't, don't you, Detective?"

"Unusual?"

"My apologies. That was the wrong word. Unlikely. Within six hours we have discovered her flat mate – lovers. One dead and one almost dead."

"Two murder attempts?"

"Could be. Or maybe Zoe had something to do with the death of Pippa and then tried to commit suicide."

Konsa nodded enthusiastically, his double chin wobbling. "Yes, that makes sense..."

Davies cut him off before he went down the proverbial rabbit hole. "Or perhaps she had nothing to do with Pippa's death but found out and then tried to commit suicide."

Again, Konsa latched onto the idea. Davies could see it in his eyes. Eager to close the case. Eager to impress a DCI from the UK. Inwardly Davies sighed. "But if that was the case, why wouldn't she call for help? Call an ambulance for Pippa? And why would she handcuff herself? Doesn't add up."

Konsa's face said it all. Hope of a quick case closure dashed immediately. "The man, Balague, he said that the two girls seemed happy. That they never argued. Their relationship was hidden – people just assumed they were roommates."

"I didn't realise that they shared the flat?" Davies said, surprised.

"Not officially they didn't. Zoe was new this year and so the new staff get the... less nice rooms and the returning staff get the better ones. It would seem that Zoe had befriended Pippa to the point that she spent a lot of her time in the nicer flat. It is common here."

"Interesting. Did Balague mention anyone else that visited or stayed in the flat?"

"No, but he said that his shifts are not the same as the girls. People could have come to the flat and he would not know."

Davies scratched at the stubble on his chin, unused to the growth. "We have multiple possibilities here, but I think we can safely assume that they are linked, yes?"

"Yes," Konsa agreed.

"I can dust the flat for prints if you would like while Doctor Karagounis finishes the autopsy and the print checks from the original crime scene."

"Yes, if you can?" Konsa said solemnly "I am sorry we do not have any more..."

He was interrupted by his phone ringing. "Sorry," he mumbled, holding up his phone in apology.

Davies waved him away and went back to the scene. His gut said that this wasn't a suicide, but perhaps made to look like one. More subterfuge just like the crime at the beach? Perhaps. It would all be so much easier if Zoe could regain consciousness.

Dusting the place for prints was a daunting task. He knew how to do it but was far from experienced or quick. Luckily, Konsa came to the rescue.

"The extra officers I had requested have arrived from Crete. They will be here in thirty minutes. One of the team is a member of the forensics team, so they can do this place."

"Excellent. They would be far better than I. Once they've done a sweep, I'd like to look around if that's ok with you Detective?"

Konsa shrugged "Ok. I do not see what you think you will find, but if it makes you happy, you may look."

A curt nod of thanks was all Davies had to offer. "I think I will go back to the hotel. See if reception can make a call to the hospital to see how Zoe is doing."

Konsa lit up a cigarette, blowing the blue-tinged smoke into the air. Davies grimaced.

Konsa grinned. "Everyone in Greece smokes."

Just like the vodka lie, Davies suspected that wasn't strictly true. "Enjoy the fag. I'm off."

Disgusting habit.

Davies returned to the hotel, dropping in on reception. They promised to keep on trying to get hold of the hospital, telling him it was always hard to reach them. Davies thanked them and made his way back down to the beach. He wanted to look at the pizza parlour again. He knew he'd missed something. It nibbled away at his grey matter like a mouse at Swiss cheese.

Yeah, and your brain is leaking like its full of holes too, old man.

Davies stood in the parlour, his back to the oven which gave him a first-class view of the sea. At least it would have if it wasn't for all the overweight holiday makers turning their pasty white skin into varying shades of red. Almost everyone had food or a drink in their hands. Greek pittas and beer seemed to be the most common choice, with the odd cocktail being swished around. It continually amazed Davies at just how unfit the general public was. An all-inclusive hotel didn't exactly seem like the right place to be if you struggled with your weight. Still, it made him feel a whole lot better about his own physique.

Concentrate man.

He started by studiously scanning the end of the parlour that he had done earlier and came out happy that he'd not missed anything. Working his way down to the other end where Konsa searched, he peered under the top shelves where jars of pizza sauce were neatly arranged along with packets of cardboard pizza slice holders. Ducking down onto his haunches, he

94

spotted another shelf with bags of flour and half of the shelf was refrigerated and contained premade dough. Behind him was another fridge with packets of cheese – grated and sliced depending on the type.

He was just about to get up when something caught his eye. Down in the corner, to the right of the cheese fridge. *What was that?* Light had briefly danced upon a surface. Davies snatched a napkin from the stack that sat on the counter and knelt back down.

Dammit man. Another reason to have your phone - the torch! Shit. He needed to snap a pic.

Grabbing the closest lifeguard, he commandeered his phone amongst hearty protests. He snapped the scene.

Stretching out with his right arm, bracing with his left, his fingers reached something hard and cylindrical. He gently pulled it out from its hiding place.

A pizza cutter. What was it doing down there?

Bringing it back into the light, Davies studied it closely, taking photos from every angle, the lifeguard now more intrigued than annoyed.

What's that?

Davies was caught between a triumphant grin and frustrated grimace. Right there, on the edge of the cutting wheel there was small amount of dried red liquid. Pizza sauce perhaps, but in all his years on the job, he'd seen a lot of blood and he was certain when he saw it.

Could it be the clue he'd been searching for?

He carefully placed the cutter in one of the cardboard pizza slice holders, took a close-up photo of the suspected blood and hurried off with it to get hold of Karagounis. The arriving team from Crete were closer, but right now, he trusted the doctor with this vital evidence.

Chapter Seven

Things were different in Kos and Davies was struggling to deal with that. He'd retrieved his phone from his room, in theory connecting him to the world, but he couldn't get hold of the hospital. He couldn't get hold of Doctor Karagounis. He couldn't get hold of Detective Konsa. It was eternally frustrating, and all this while, he was supposed to be on holiday.

So, as if he was on holiday, he ordered a coffee and tried to relax, the last of the sun worshippers retreating from the loungers around the pool, heading to the bar for a pre-shower drink. Of course, that would be followed by a post shower/pre dinner drink or two. A drink with dinner. Then it went onto the evening drinking because, well, they were on holiday!

Davies had to admit, an espresso martini this evening was tempting, but for now he sipped at his strong coffee.

Where was everyone? Why wouldn't the hospital respond? So frustrating.

The comings and goings of the hotel passed him by while he mulled over the case he'd somehow become embroiled in.

A coach pulled up at the drop-off point just in front of the hotel. Davies could see through the glass fronted reception that they were not new arrivals, but existing guests that had probably been out on a day trip somewhere. The local rep – a Scotsman called Dougie – had tried his best to entice Davies into signing up. He had to admit that the 'three island tour' sounded pretty good, but he was long past those package trips. He preferred to go alone. Two families and a good-looking couple poured through the front door looking tired and sun kissed. It hadn't been that sunny today, so he presumed they'd been out on a boat, and it was the wind that had coloured their cheeks.

One of the children, a snotty little boy who couldn't have been more than four years old, was crying. No, not crying. It was somewhere between a screech, a scream and a phlegm-spewing shout. It was a fucking awful sound. Davies was drawn to the couple who were last through the door. You could tell by their faces that the sounds this kid made were nothing new.

Jeez. How long had they had to listen to that?

The coach pulled away and a pair of quad bikes pulled through and went past the glazed frontage.

Ah, that's more like it. Davies had been drawn to the quad bikes as a cheap and fun way to explore the island.

You could rent them from within the hotel. There were usually two men sat at a desk further down the foyer. One rented cars, the other quad bikes and funny, little dune-buggy-type machines as well as those death-trap scooters.

He craned his neck to see two people he recognised from around the bars traipse through the door. Helmet hair betrayed what they'd been up to, and the wide grins confirmed that it had been a good day. He watched them walk over to hand the keys back and the man who hired the bikes stood to greet them.

What was that?

The man, tall with slick backed hair and a yellow gold chain round his neck winced and clutched at his side towards the bottom of his ribs as he accepted the keys.

Interesting. What happen to you, son?

Davies watched. The grimace quickly turned into a smile. He said something to the pair of riders, presumably something along the lines of, "Did you have fun?"

People walked in front of them, obscuring Davies view so he stood, picked up the pizza cutter, which was now safely ensconced in a clear plastic bag, and took a few paces closer.

That's better.

The man waved the riders off, who were no doubt heading for a shower before grabbing a celebratory drink or two. The quad-hire man, dark denim trousers and a green polo shirt that displayed the company name on the left breast, gingerly sat down. He winced once again, his right hand reaching down to cradle his left side. Finally seated, he puffed out his cheeks and breathed out heavily.

Something inside Davies' head rang. His interest sparked.

Then his phone rang, making him jump.

"Hello?" he replied, not recognising the number.

"DCI Davies?" came the seductive voice of the doctor. "You were trying to contact me?"

"I was... everything ok?"

"Sorry. My phone died and I've just plugged it in and saw that I had missed calls from this number."

"Yes, I see. Um, what number is this? Where are you?"

"This is the number for my lab."

"Excellent. How are things going?" He sounded like an idiot. Not professional.

She's pretty, and you're struggling with that. Embarrassing.

"Well, DCI Davies, the autopsy is finished. She was in good health, and I can confirm that death was caused by suffocation. Suffocated by, it appears, from sand being forced into her mouth, blocking her airway. Sand in the lungs and in the stomach confirm this."

"How do you know it was forced?"

"Bruising that had not come out because she died so soon after it was inflicted is evidenced around the jawbone and neck."

"I see. No prints?"

"None."

"And the print I sent you?"

"One hundred percent match with the victim."

Really? So she was in the pizza parlour. The shoes weren't taken there. They must have been put there as a matter of convenience as much as a plan to burn them.

"But why were they removed? It makes littles sense." Davies mused out loud.

"I agree. However, having worn similar shoes, they are easily slipped off."

"Hmmm. Interesting. Not removed, but perhaps they came off in the act of moving the body?"

"It is possible, yes" Karagounis agreed.

"Excellent work, Doctor. I'm afraid I have another task for you."

"If it's the crime scene from the flat, that's being taken care of by another team."

Davies detected something in her voice. Frustration? Annoyance? "I understand. No, this is from the Pizza Parlour again."

"I thought you and Detective Konsa had cleared the area?"

"So did I, but on return to the scene, I found something else. Can you do blood work?"

"DNA check you mean? Of course. I may be a one-person band, but I have the ability."

Davies blushed. He'd upset her. "I'm sorry, I didn't mean to offend..."

Karagounis sighed. "No, no. It is me. Being too defensive. I know what you mean. I need to come back to the hotel, anyway. I have a portable machine I can bring with me, which I can hook up to the hotels secure network and check the database. How's thirty minutes sound?"

"Fantastic. See you shortly, Doctor" He hung up, quickly realising that he was grinning like a teenager who'd found their first love.

To hell with it. When this is over, ask her out to dinner. Eleanor has moved on after all.

Pocketing his phone, he placed the pizza roller bag in the safe at reception and headed over to ask some questions about quadbikes.

A pair of German lads in the early thirties wearing garish Golf attire had beaten Davies to the front of the queue, and so he had to wait.

No problem. I've got all night.

Five minutes later, the two golfers left with the booking form for a dune buggy rental the very next day. Davies politely stepped aside.

"Danke," the shorter of the two said.

Polite fella, but that golf club jumper is awful, lad. "Bitte Schön," he said in his best accent.

"Whoooaaa! That is good, ya!" the taller one exclaimed, beaming ear to ear.

Been on the beer then.

Davies duly returned the smile and took the vacated seat in front of the rental guy.

The man scribbled something on the pad in front of him and murmured, "One moment, please."

Davies sat quietly, studying the man who eventually raised his ever-so-slightly balding head to meet Davies' gaze. "Hello, how may I help you?" His name badge now clear to see – Joao.

He was of medium height but had the broad shoulders of a swimmer. Lean and no doubt agile without the injury, he cut a handsome figure, if coming towards the end of his prime. No doubt he did well with the women that came through the hotel looking for a little holiday romance.

"Hi, buddy. I'm looking at renting something for the day to explore the island. What have you got?"

"Ah. A fine idea, sir." The politeness felt forced yet well practiced. "When were you thinking of venturing out from the hotel?"

Hah! The salesman. It's just a dry island.

Davies wasn't fussed. "Tomorrow maybe?"

"No problem, sir. Tomorrow we only have these quads available." He span a laminated sheet around for Davies to see. There were all the vehicles that were depicted on the flyer, each with a daily hire price. He pointed at a red and black quad. "I give you for fifty-five for the day." It was sixty on the listing.

Davies feigned interest, acting out the tourist. "Aren't they dangerous?" he asked sheepishly.

Joao chuckled. "No sir, not all. There is strictly no off roading in our vehicles. These quads are stable and comfy. A man like you will have no problems."

"And they come with a helmet?"

"Of course sir! All included in the sixty euros"

"Didn't you just say fifty-five...?"

Joao showed no signs of apology or embarrassment at the supposed mistake "Yes, yes. Fifty-five for you, sir."

"I am interested. Would you be able to show me one before I agree?"

The smile faltered a moment. "I am afraid they are very dirty, and I carry a little injury. I assure you that they are safe. In the morning we will show you all the controls. No problem. So, fifty-five for tomorrow?"

Davies had no intention whatsoever of renting the damn thing. He just wanted to see how badly injured Joao was. "Oh, how did you injure yourself? Not on a quad bike I hope?!" He laid it on thick.

"I er, no. It was a, er..."

Joao's awkward story was shelved because Konsa chose that very moment to arrive and loom large over the desk.

Dammit!

"DCI Davies," Konsa said, his voice stern.

Davies just caught Joao's eyes bulge at the mention of his title. *Interesting.*

"Hello, Detective Konsa," Davies replied as warmly as he could. Joao kept a flat face this time. *He must know who Konsa is.*

Konsa continued with total disregard for the salesman. "I have just received word from the hospital. The woman is in recovery. There is damage to her lungs, but she will live."

Davies was delighted. "That's great news," he said, the pride in what he had done shone through. He'd saved someone's life. Again. "Can we speak to her?"

"I am afraid that she is still unconscious"

"Of course. I understand." Davies had to reign it in. "No problem. The Doctor will be here soon. I have something for her."

Konsa's brows lifted "Really? What is that?"

Davies made his apologies to Joao, suddenly aware that he was discussing a case in front a member of public.

"Of course. Of course." Joao said with a politely dismissive wave of his hand.

Davies stood and pulled Konsa away from the desk and over to a quiet corner. "I found some more evidence. It may have a print."

"Where did you find this evidence? What is it?" Konsa seemed annoyed.

So you should be. You missed it!

"It's a pizza cutting wheel. It was down by the fridges in the pizza parlour.

"Really? That wasn't there before," Konsa said, still dismissive

"I don't know what to say. It was definitely there that I found it. I'm waiting for the doctor to arrive so we can do a blood trace on it."

"There is blood?"

"Or pizza sauce, yes. Again, we will know more when the..."

Konsa's demeanour changed drastically "No, No. You are on holiday. I will take care of it. Where is it?"

"I really don't mind."

"It is ok. You go shower and get ready for your dinner and drinks. You like the doctor, yes?"

Davies was caught totally off guard. "I er..."

"She a very pretty woman. This is normal. You go make yourself smart, and I will meet the Doctor. When you come down, she will be finished, and you can have a drink with her, yes?" A grimy smile spread across his face.

You can keep your hands off her mate.

"Well..."

"Just give me the evidence, Davies, and I will sort it." He held out his hand, waiting.

"Well, I'm not carrying it around, am I?"

Who does he think he is?

"Of course not. I meant no, how you say in England, harm?"

Davies sighed. He was tired and hungry. Evidently his patience was suffering.

"Ok. Sorry, Detective. I think I do need that shower. The evidence is in the reception safe."

"No problem. You go and I will retrieve it. They know me here."

"If you're sure?"

"Of course! Go and get ready for the doctor! Show her some English charm!" Konsa laughed heartily, slapping him on the back. Davies couldn't help but think he was being laughed *at*.

He gave up the argument and headed off to his room. He really did want to be presentable to Karagounis. It was a nice feeling.

Chapter 8

After a quick shower and a scrub of his teeth, Davies almost skipped down the stairs on his way to reception to meet the doctor... and Detective Konsa, he guessed.

To his self-contained delight, Dr Karagounis sat nursing a mug of steaming liquid on one of the sofas that decorated the reception area of the hotel. She had changed since the morning; professional yet feminine. She wore dark tight fitting combat trousers with tan ankle height walking boots. Her loose-fitting navy blouse hung seductively over a navy sports top. Her hair was pulled back into a neat ponytail. A fresh application of subtle makeup managed to mask some of the exhaustion she clearly felt.

In many ways she was a mirror image of himself. Light grey combats, tan walking boots and black and red checked shirt. He flet comfortable, but unlike the doctor, he hadn't applied any makeup to hide the grey bags under his eyes.

A quick scan of the reception showed no signs of the Greek detective or Joao. He fixed a genuine smile to his face and approached the doctor. She didn't notice him approaching. She appeared to be studying the contents of her mug.

"Reading tea leaves, doctor? Has it come to that?" Davies asked, breaking her concentration.

"Sorry?" she said, startled and confused.

Davies grinned. "Your tea? Has the medical profession taken up a new way of analysing evidence? Tea leaf reading?"

Karagounis glanced down at her mug and back at him, understanding dawning on her "Very good, DCI Davies. the leaves want to know where this piece of evidence you want me to analyse, is?"

Annoyance must have flashed across his face because the doctor was quick to add "But of course, you are on holiday, and this is all very much an intrusion..."

He didn't let her finish, ashamed that she thought he was annoyed at her. "No, no not all. That wasn't it. Detective Konsa assured me that he'd meet you and hand it over. I take it that he hasn't?"

The doctor shook her head. "Sorry. I've not seen him."

"I'm starting to see what you were inferring to when we first met. Never mind. I'll go and retrieve it now. One moment."

Fucking useless excuse for a cop.

Davies marched over to the reception desk, trying to shake the annoyance, aware that it was not the fault of the staff or the doctor. "Hello," he greeted the first available staff member. The young woman was different from the one that had placed the pizza cutter in the safe. They must have changed over for the night shift. "Earlier, one of your colleagues placed something in the safe for me. Could I retrieve it please?"

"Certainly, sir," the young woman said with a smile. She was incredibly short and could barely see over the desk. "What room number are you?"

"A room number wasn't required. It was held there for the police."

A flash of concern appeared, but she duly turned and went through the same door her colleague had gone through to place it in the safe.

After a ridiculously long two-minute wait, the young woman reappeared, unease written all over her face. "I am sorry, sir, but the safe is empty."

Dumbstruck, all Davies could do was repeat what he'd just heard. "Empty?"

"Yes sir. We currently have nothing in our safe."

"But I only had it placed there an hour ago!"

She looked very uncomfortable. "I'm sorry sir, but I don't know what to tell you other that the fact that it's empty. Do you know who put it in there for you?"

His head was running at warp speed trying to figure out what had happened here. "Her name was Tanya I think? Has Detective Konsa been here? Did he ask to take something from the safe?"

"No, sir. I haven't seen the detective, although I only started thirty minutes ago. I think you mean Tamina? I have her number. I will call her to ask about your item. Is that ok?"

"Yes. Yes please. I'll wait."

"Very well," she said, politeness personified.

The young woman, who went by the name of Marina, picked up a mobile phone from her desk and quickly dialled a number.

Davies leant against the desk and tried to nonchalantly turn to check on the doctor. She was staring at him.

Checking me out or checking on me?

He smiled back and gave a shrug of the shoulders in the form of an apology.

She smiled back, understanding.

He'd been wrapped up in his little flirting that he hadn't heard Marina on the phone "Excuse me, sir?"

"Sorry," Davies apologised, turning back to face the young receptionist. "What did Tamina say?"

"She confirmed that she placed your item in the safe. She also said that the detective was here just before we changed over shifts."

"And did he retrieve my item from the safe?"

"I am sorry, but she said that she didn't remove it, but she said that he may have the code for the safe."

"He what?"

"He is the island's detective, Mr Davies."

Detective or not, he shouldn't have the hotel safe code. *Did he take it?*

"Okay. Thank you for your help, Marina."

"You're welcome, sir."

Thankful that he'd remembered his phone for once, he pulled it from his pocket and dialled the number that Konsa had given him. It went straight to voicemail.

Dammit!

Frowning, he retraced his footsteps to the doctor who had finished her tea but cupped the mug in both hands for warmth.

Bloody boiling in here. How can she be cold?

"A problem?" she asked, one eyebrow raised.

Davies was initially unsure how to approach the current situation. He was a guest here, but it also allowed him to be objective. "I'm sorry to report, Doctor, that the evidence that I asked you over to identify is no longer here."

Eyebrow still raised. "And where might it be?"

Davies winced. "There is every chance that Detective Konsa has it, although his whereabouts are currently a mystery."

"But you asked Detective Konsa to give it to me, yes?"

Am I reading into things that aren't there?

"I did, yes. What I don't like is that the reception staff didn't have to retrieve it for him – he knows the safe code. Something isn't right here."

"May I ask what the evidence was?"

"It was a pizza cutter, and it appeared to have blood on it."

Karagounis frowned. "That is certainly something I'd like to see. There could be two things there. Possible prints on the handle and obviously the blood work on the blade, I assume?"

"Correct," he confirmed while keeping an eye out for the errant detective.

Davies took a seat at the other end of the sofa, keeping a respectful distance, even though he desperately wanted to move closer. He caught a whiff of her perfume. He had no idea what brand that was, but he knew what he liked, and it seemed that the doctor had a good nose for knowing what went well with her skin. "Things aren't falling into place yet. I have all these threads that my mind is pulling at, but they keep ending in knots. Some probably have nothing to do with the case at all."

"Would it help to talk these through? The threads, I mean?"

Davies considered it a minute.

What the hell.

"Okay. Good idea, thanks." He paused to try and put his thoughts in some kind of order.

"Right, So I think that Pippa was murdered down at the beach. I think she and her assailant were in or near the pizza parlour. The shoes were hastily put in the oven – because they kept coming off as she was dragged, under the arms, as you mentioned. The lack of bruising suggests that she was unconscious when sand was pushed into her mouth. He or she just needed to keep her mouth open. She was then dragged to the poolside beach and the sand there was used to mislead us, however temporarily."

"I agree so far," The doctor murmured. "But I would suggest that the initial sand – the sand that was ingested, was forced in when she *was* conscious. My guess would be that she was just purely overpowered. Perhaps the weight of her attacker was enough? For her to have swallowed the sand..."

"And leave no bruising?"

Karagounis shrugged "If someone the size of you or Konsa were to sit on me, I'd have little hope of pushing you off."

Davies pondered the suggestion for a moment. *She's good.*

"Okay, I see what you're saying. Thank you." he said with a smile. "Now, the possibly missing evidence. I think that it will point us towards the attacker. If we get hold of it, we will find that Pippa's prints will come up on the handle and the blood will be of the killers. It got batted away and fell behind the fridge and forgotten about in the hurry to move the body."

Karagounis nodded along with the story.

"Now, we have the unfortunate girl in the hospital. A roommate. A lover. A witness?"

"What is her name, if you don't mind me asking?"

"Zoe... Apologies, I am unaware of her surname."

"I know her. She was dating a man who works here."

"Interesting. The neighbour said that they were sexually liberal. Who was she dating?"

Karagounis twisted in her seat and pointed. "Him."

Davies jaw dropped. She was pointing at Joao the quadbike man who'd returned to his little desk. "Holy shit" He breathed "That makes sense. I think, Doctor, that you might just..." He tailed off.

Joao had noticed the interest Davies and the Doctor were paying him and hurriedly began to clear his desk.

Davies rose from his seat and quickly walked over to the desk where Joao was now beginning to move away.

"Joao!" Davies said, authority hanging off the name. "I need to ask you some questions..."

Panic shone in Joao's eyes, and he darted towards the main hotel doors.

"Wait!" Davies shouted. "POLICE! STOP!"

Joao ignored the instruction, shoving an elderly couple out of his way, making for the main entrance door that swished open upon his approach. He had to pause briefly for the delay in the door's response, but he was out into the Greek night before Davies had covered half the ground.

Davies quickened his pace, pausing to check that the elderly couple were okay before pushing through the same door Joao had used. He saw Joao climb aboard one of his quadbikes and start her up. The engine roared and he twisted the throttle, the bike lurching forward.

"STOP!" Davies cried. He dared not jump in the way as the bike sped past and out towards the exit. Davies ran towards the other bikes and started checking the ignitions. NO keys!

He heard rushed footsteps behind him. Spinning round, fists raised, he was greeted by the doctor, cheeks flushed. She was holding up some keys. "He left these on the desk!"

What a woman!

"Do you know which one they belong to?" he asked, desperation leaking into his voice.

"Fob has seven on it."

They both scanned the fleet of five quads and quickly found number seven. To their surprise and good fortune, it was the frontmost bike. Davies held out his hand for the keys. "If you please, doctor."

She handed the keys over as she passed him and popped open the luggage box that had been fitted to the rear. She pulled out two bike helmets while Davies swung his leg over the bike. He found the ignition, slid the key into the well lubricated barrel and turned it. The engine roared into life before settling into an aggressive idle, just as he felt the bike gently lean to one side. Twisting, he found Karagounis climbing aboard.

"No, no, no," he shook his head.

In silent response she handed him a black helmet which he took. He watched her pull her ponytail out, shaking her hair loose and slipping the blue helmet on over her head with a grace he did not think possible.

"If you don't hurry up, we'll lose him!" she shouted over the growling engine.

With no time to argue he pulled the black lid over his head. "Please, just hold on," he demanded, his eyes angry yet pleading.

She gave him a reassuring smile in return.

Their bike didn't have a twist throttle. Instead, it had a user-friendly trigger set beneath the right handle grip. A quick scan of the setup directed him to a simple auto gear selector that he pushed into drive. He used his right thumb to gently push the throttle and the bike crept forward. He felt the doctor knees brace against him from behind. Reassured that she was holding on, he gave the throttle a little more power and the bike took off.

Wow!

They set off, the main hotel quickly behind them. They rounded a corner and up over the brow of a hill. This road ran in front of the sister hotel that the doctor was based in. Gawping guests watched as they sped past and rounded another corner that dropped into a valley. They couldn't see the other quad in front of them, but there was only one road in and out of the hotels' resort. At the bottom of the hill sat a security checkpoint with a man wildly waving his arms at them to slow down. Davies did as the man instructed, but not because he was going to stop, but because the right turn was tight, and he didn't want to topple the bike, especially with his precious cargo hanging on behind him.

Karagounis leaned in and shouted, "WHY DID HE RUN?"

Concentrating hard, Davies shouted "I NOTICED THAT HE HAD AN INJURED TORSO. I NOW THINK THAT IS FROM AN ATTACK."

"FROM THE PIZZA CUTTER?"

"EXACTLY."

"OH MY GOD!"

Davies eased off the throttle as they approached a fork in the road. To the left, the tarmac continued and headed off the main town. To the right was a dirt track that climbed up and away from the hotel.

"Which way?" Davies asked, no longer shouting. He couldn't see the quad anywhere.

While they tried to decide, the doctor shouted and pointed "There!"

Davies followed the direction of her pointing hand. She was indicating up the into the mountain. Davies couldn't see what had made her point that way. As if reading his mind, she barked "Headlights! Very quick! He must be climbing the old mountain pass!"

"You're sure?" He asked, eyeing the much more welcoming tarmac.

"Yes! I think he's flicking his headlights on and off. Balancing vision with trying to be covert."

She shouted, confidence oozing from her voice.

He had no reason to question her again. There weren't any headlights on the winding tarmac road that led to town. It had to the be the mountain track.

Dammit.

"HOLD ON!" he shouted, turning to the right and giving the bike some throttle. The road began its rapid decline in quality almost immediately with the tarmac gone. Truck tracks and flood water ravines made up the shape of the single track. Loose stones and rocks littered the surface. Anything less than a four-wheel drive vehicle was never going to make it up here. The track wound left and right, their headlights lighting up the darkness before them.

Soon, a white building came into view. Davies assumed it was the old church that you could see from the hotel. The small church was on their left as they roared past it, chunky tyres spitting loose stone and dust into the air, the bike fighting for traction. The glimpse Davies had of the church revealed that it appeared to be well kept and used, despite its odd placement and appearance from afar.

How the hell is he navigating this without light?

In answer, up ahead, a light flashed on for the briefest of moments. "THERE!" Karagounis shouted, risking her balance by letting go with her right hand to once again point up into the mountainside.

"I SEE IT!" Davies shouted back, now glad that he'd trusted her. The road dipped down for a stretch before rising once again and turning left into the mountain. The road tracked round, following the cut of the terrain. They had to slow where there had been a rockfall. Davies presumed that this was where Joao had used his lights. Even if you knew the track, there was no way you'd be able to navigate the pass without some light to guide the way.

Frustration built with the slow pace, but he was unwilling to risk their lives. "WHERE DOES THE ROAD LEAD?" he shouted over his shoulder.

"I don't know! I've only been so far. As far as the point that looks back out over the hotel!"

Clear of the rock fall, Davies gave the bike more throttle and pushed it further up the pass. Over the roar of the engine, they both heard a crash.

Shit! Was that him?

In response, Davies gave the trigger a little more pressure and their speed increased, adrenaline surging through his veins. Rounding another corner, still climbing, their headlights picked out stacked stones. They looked like little memorials. They were all on the apex of a bend.

"THAT'S AS FAR AS I'VE BEEN!" Karagounis shouted.

Approaching the stacks of stones, they saw the fibreglass trim that matched the colours of Joao's quadbike sat awkwardly on the track.

He must have hit them.

Davies slowed, clocking the trail of fluid that marked the dried surface of the track. Now they had a trail to follow. Davies slowed, wary of the same fate as the man they chased. The edge of the mountain road to their right fell away steeply, offering anyone that fell an almost certain death ending in a burial at sea. The light of the moon that had rapidly risen over the mountain failed to properly illuminate the point where the cliff disappeared.

Davies shuddered. It had been years since he last drove quickly with someone he cared for under his protection.

Cared for?

He shook the idea from his thoughts and concentrated on the surface that could be called a road with less and less certainty the further they climbed. It ducked back into the mountain face once again, tracking a gorge. There was a tight right turn where someone had built a small bridge to cover the gap in the natural mountain face that had so far offered a route. Davies slowed even more to navigate the turn, easing the powerful quad back onto safer ground. Ahead was another turn to the left. They had no idea what was held in store for them round that bend, so he kept his speed low.

The road cut sharply into the rockface. A huge overhang blocked out what little moonlight there was.

Davies realised too late.

His headlights picked out the stricken quadbike, trim hanging off at an awkward angle. He barely had time to register the riderless vehicle.

Something hard smashed into his chest.

The impact slammed him backwards into his pillion passenger.

His grip gone from the handles, the revs died off his vehicle, but its forward momentum continued while he and the doctor went backwards. They were a mess of limbs clattering harshly to the rocky ground.

His muffled cry was masked by the scream that cut through him.

Doc!

What had hit them? He rolled to his side, trying desperately not to land anymore unintentional blows upon the no doubt seriously injured doctor.

The irony.

He rolled and sprang onto his feet in a low crouch, eyes scanning, grappling for some semblance of night vision. Movement ahead. Approaching.

"Don't come any closer!" Davies threatened, the strength in his voice masking the fear that he felt.

The attacker faltered for half a step, but no more. He had something in his hands. Short, but not shaped like a baseball bat.

A groan from behind him. He risked a quick a look. The doctor laid in a crumpled mess against the mountainside, her left arm protruding at a horribly unnatural angle. She was alive though. For now.

Switching his attention back to the attacker, the moonlight had shifted again, and it was plain to see that it was Joao, and he was holding a splintered branch in his hands.

That's what must have hit me.

The impact must have broken the branch. Davies' lucky day.

"Don't come any closer, Joao! It's not worth it!" It was then that he realised the helmet he had worn was no longer atop his head. The result of not having time to have done up the chin strap. More luck.

Joao stopped two metres away and sneered. "Or what, old man? What are you going to do?"

"I've had combat training, young man. You may have taken us by surprise, but I *will* take you down if you step any closer."

That was a LONG time ago, man.

He must have said it with enough bravado because Joao hesitated, unsure. "You're lying, old man. I'm gonna fuck you up."

Davies changed tact. "Why did you kill Pippa?"

Joao still hadn't moved any closer, and this new question unsettled him more.

"Fucking dyke," he growled. "Both of them."

"Why did you kill her?" Davies was stalling, looking for a way out.

Insulted, Joao spread his arms like a gladiator soaking up the roars of adulation from a crowd. "Men are the powerful ones. Women just need to scrub, cook, obey and service us men!" His statement needed no more expansion, but he thrust his hands towards his groin, making it clear what he meant.

Pig.

"So, this was all just because your girl liked the taste of women more than you?"

Joao turned angry again, done with his pelvic thrusts. "Fuck you are? How dare you? Weak English coming over here! Bet you're fucking gay!"

Ridiculous ravings of a nut job as it were, Davies couldn't help but flick a furtive glance towards the injured Karagounis. It was enough for Joao to have seen though.

"Ohhhh. Not gay at all! You wanna fuck the doctor, eh?" he licked his lips grotesquely. "Yeah, I'd like a bit of that tasty arse. Hot for an old bitch."

Anger flared in Davies stomach. It was a feeling he hadn't felt in a long time.

131

"You'd better shut that mouth of yours," Davies growled, his muscle fibres tensing, ready for action.

Joao threw back his head and laughed evilly. "You?" he said, incredulous. "Don't be so fucking stupid. I'm gonna rip that stupid head off your shoulders!"

Davies watched as his quadbike completed its final journey, rolling to the edge of the road and tipping over the edge, crashing down the mountainside.

The distraction was just enough for Davies to make his move, lunging, catching the homophobic monster off guard. He hit the man low with his right shoulder, knocking the wind out of the bastard. Joao dropped the remains of his weapon upon impact, the wind rushing out of him with an audible 'whoosh' before he hit the ground, Davies crashing down onto him.

They struggled in a heap, each grappling for a decent hold on the other. Untrained scrapping from both men. Close quarter punches failed to land and neither showed any sign of holding the upper hand. They rolled over, loose stones digging into ribs and skin, dust collecting in eyes and noses.

Both men grunted with the effort, a fight or die desperation eeking into their actions. Davies began to tire, the extra years he had on his opponent beginning to show despite his exercise regimen.

Joao rolled and straddled the older man. He began to throw wild punches towards Davies' face.

Davies held up his arms in defence, the brief foray into boxing coming back to him in his hour of need. None of the blows did any damage, with only the odd fist squirming through on a deflection and not causing Davies any real discomfort.

Joao's attack slowed and Davies saw his opportunity. His right hand fell and grappled at the loose road beneath him, quickly wrapping his hands around the first candidate for what he sought. He brough the dusty stone up in an awkward arc, but with enough force to cause damage.

The rock connected with the area at the bottom of Joao's ribs where Davies had seen him struggle earlier. The spot where Pippa must have sliced him with the pizza cutter. Joao howled in pain and his weight shifted, giving Davies enough time shove his attacker off him.

Davies leapt to his feet as agile as he had ever done and rounded on the injured man. He kicked out at him, catching him between buttock and lower back. More agonising cries came from the bastard. That didn't stop Davies aiming another kick at him, this one connecting with the arm that clutched the wounded ribs. Another howl. Davies was gripped by anger, the red mist clouding his thoughts.

"Get up!" he yelled at the now cowering man. "Get up and face me!"

"Who do you think you are, man?" Joao dragged himself to his feet, confidence returning when he realised that Davies wouldn't finish him. "You can't touch me! I have friends. Powerful friends, you hear!" Spittle flew from his bloodied mouth.

The bravado didn't stop him from edging backwards when Davies took a step closer, his hands still balled into fists.

"Nobody can save you," said Davies through gritted teeth. "You are going to prison for a long time."

He took another step towards the nervous Joao who in turn stepped backwards, intent on keeping the six-foot gap between them.

"This isn't your island man. You're nobody here. I'll be okay. Joao is always ok! I have friends, man!"

His ever-wilder taunts and claims were cut short as both men looked up, distracted by a high-pitched whine.

What's that?

Before either man had a chance to react, a high-powered drone came flying low up the dirt road, the now distinctive whine deafening in such close quarters. The drone flattened out and flew at them, the wash of the small yet powerful blades catching Davies across the face, kicking up dust into his eyes.

Although vision compromised, he saw everything unfold.

The drone, at whatever high speed it was doing crashed straight into Joao's chest, the impact sickening, despite the lightweight construction of the unit.

Joao stumbled backwards, unbalanced by the impact. His left heel caught a stone and he toppled backwards, fear and shock etched onto his face.

As one they toppled out into the abyss that was the picturesque backdrop of the Aegean Sea.

The moonlight lit up his face, his eyes searching in desperation for a way out, the realisation never quite having time to register as he disappeared over the edge, wrapped up in the broken drone.

An anguished scream cut through the night, the last sounds the killer would ever make.

Even if Davies had wanted to reach out and attempt to save him, there wasn't time. The space between them was too great. The speed of the attack too quick.

Davies, reactions delayed, threw himself to the ground and crawled towards the Doctor. "Doc!" He shouted, fear gripping the edges of the words.

Please be ok!

He reached the battered and bruised woman, seeing her chest rise and fall.

Thank God.

Then a weak voice "Davies? Is that you?"

Emotions he hadn't felt in a long time flooded through his system. He carefully wrapped an arm around her "Your arm...?"

"Broken," she said through gritted teeth. Then "Joao?"

"Gone."

She wasn't interested in how, just a sense of relief in her laboured breathing at the news.

"Your chest," Davies said, worry in every syllable "Another injury?"

"Cracked or broken ribs I think." She grimaced. "Next time, Davies, I'll drive."

Davies smiled. If this situation ever happened again, he would gladly be the cushion she fell on.

"Call me Antony, eh?"

They both smiled, looked up at the moon and enjoyed the painful yet satisfying moment.

Chapter Nine

The Hellenic Rescue team had mobilised from Kos town and liaised with the doctor via mobile phone throughout their forty-minute journey down to Kardemena. It was clear that her injuries would make getting back down the mountain extremely difficult and they pushed to commandeer a helicopter to lift her off the mountain. She vehemently refused, claiming that it was a waste of money and resources. If the team could get a buggy to them along with some powerful painkillers, she would be ok to get back down. Despite their protests, she won the argument and they agreed to take two of Joao's dune buggies with just two team members – one to drive each buggy.

While they waited, looking at the stricken quadbike Joao had ridden up and subsequently broken, they discussed the day's events.

Through intermittently grated teeth Karagounis asked lots of questions. "Do you think that Joao killed Pippa and tried to murder Zoe?"

"It's possible... probable, but I don't have anything to pin him to either scene. Without that pizza cutter and what we think is his DNA, we can't even put Pippa's death down to him. I mean, the pieces add up, but without the cutter..." Davies let out a dejected sigh.

So close.

"Why do you think Konsa has disappeared with the evidence?" she asked.

"Again, we can't say for sure that he has. Granted, the staff saw him in the area of reception – and so they should as I told him to collect the evidence. They also claim he knows the code to the safe, but we don't know that for certain and just because we can't get hold of him now, it doesn't mean that he has run away. He may have absolutely nothing to do with any of this."

Karagounis raised her eyebrows, delicate dust filled wrinkles forming on her forehead. "You don't go along with that though, do you?"

"What do you mean?"

"I mean, Antony, you think he's involved. We have time. Talk through your theories."

She called me Antony!

He had to admit, she was spot on. "Well, things hadn't added up from the moment he got involved. Missing the pizza cutter in the parlour. There is no way he should have missed that.

139

Possibly through incompetence, but I think he saw it and ignored it. I also think that he has 100% run off with the evidence. He's either a partner in all this or he is covering for Joao."

"And the drone attack?"

"Difficult to say, isn't it? Can't be an accident, can it?"

"So Konsa flew that?"

"Or had it flown."

"But why? If he was collaborating with Joao, why would he then kill him?" She winced, the homemade sling slipping.

"Good question. You ok?"

"Yes, yes. Go on."

Davies already thought highly of the doctor in both a professional and personal capacity, but with every passing moment those feelings grew. The strength of the woman astounded him. He couldn't name many police officers who'd still be asking questions with the injuries she'd sustained. "I don't know. Something changed. The only time that I've seen them together was when Konsa told me that Zoe was still alive. Was Konsa sending Joao a message?"

"Letting him know he'd made a mistake?"

"Possibly, and that he needed to make amends...wait a minute! Shit!"

Karagounis' eyes shone, the thrill of working through a case and no doubt the adrenaline of the chase was intoxicating. "What? What have you figured out?"

Davies held up a hand asking for a moment before speaking. "What if they had been working together. Maybe, unlikely I know, Konsa was dating Zoe? Or fancied her? Maybe it's more sinister than that? What if Konsa had raped Zoe? As a pair of neanderthal men, they were insulted by the women's attraction to each other. They hatch a plan. Zoe's survival puts everything in jeopardy. Konsa decides to cover tracks and take out Joao... The Handcuffs! They were Police issue..."

Karagounis turned white as a sheet, realisation dawning.

"Zoe!" Davies exclaimed. "Konsa will go for Zoe!"

"Oh my god. Hasn't that poor girl suffered enough? You think that Konsa will try and kill Zoe in her hospital bed?"

Davies' grimace said it all. If that was Konsa controlling the drone then he had to have been piloting it from within, what, a two-mile radius? If he was heading straight for the hospital, he had a significant head start.

"You need to go. Now!" Karagounis instructed, calmness personified. Her duty of care to a patient her soul focus. "Leave me. Start off and take a buggy when you encounter the rescue team."

"But I can't leave you..."

"*GO!* A girl's life is at stake! Leave me your phone. I will call ahead. They know me. I'll tell them to not let Konsa into her room."

Davies rose up off the dusty floor and looked down on the woman for whom he realised he had a great deal of affection. Without another word, he placed his phone in her open palm and gently kissed the top of her head. She smiled, a warm and thankful smile.

Thank God for that.

Davies headed off in the dark as fast as he dared, hoping that the mountain rescue team were close and that he wasn't going to be too late.

Chapter Ten

Thankfully the rescue team weren't far off. Davies encountered them after five minutes of perilous scrambling in the dark. Initially hesitant to hand over a buggy, they finally agreed when Davies used his most authoritative police voice. Say it with confidence and people will believe you.

Twenty minutes later, he was racing along the tarmac main road that led to Kos town and the island's hospital. The usually warm air cut through his thin shirt such was his speed. If the situation had been different, this would have been an exhilarating ride. As it happened though, all he could think about was the worst-case scenario – he was too late.

He prayed that Karagounis had managed to get through to the hospital and that they listened to her. Would she have told the truth? Who could they trust? If the island's detective was bent. How many others in the force were? Davies hoped that none were involved at any level, but that would be something for the Greek internal affairs to decide.

But now it was a race. A race across an island that was sparsely populated. The unfinished blocks of apartments - victims of the pandemic's financial crush - and dusty tracks leading to tourist attractions that mostly amounted to 'ancient rubble' sped past.

Applying more pressure to the accelerator, the rear mounted engine roared, the heat warming his back. The all-terrain vehicle was unaware of the plight that Zoe faced; it was in its element.

Entering the town's outskirts, the streetlights lit his way. The rescue team had given him directions, but after the first litter of bars, restaurants and Tabacs, he picked up the international sign for hospital – a large capital H.

Screeching round a corner he leant heavily on the horn, tourists and locals alike scattered like bowling pins. He failed to apologise. His teeth were gritted in concentration.

Wouldn't hear me anyway.

He left a trail of curses and angrily waved fists as he sped towards the hospital.

Please let me be in time.

The hospital came into view. Thankfully it wasn't central to the town or on the coast itself. There weren't any security guards in the hut to tell him to slow down, but his own risk assessment dictated he do so anyway.

Abandoning the buggy across two spaces to the east of the entrance and a hundred yards away from the emergency drop off point, he took a moment to compose and come up with some kind of plan.

He was found desperately wanting. All he had to do really was get in there and protect the girl.

The wind had blown a lot of the dust off his filthy clothes, but he brushed himself down and tried to smooth his wind-swept hair in an effort to at least look vaguely presentable. Taking off at a run, he dodged past the only other people outside, a couple of grey-haired patients in dressing gowns sucking on cigarettes.

Smokers at a hospital, honestly.

The automatic doors slid open, and Davies took one last glance over his shoulder in the hope that he'd arrived before Konsa. He chided himself for not noticing what car Konsa drove.

He stepped over the threshold of the main entrance and was hit by the air conditioning, sending a chill down his already cold spine. Fixing a smile to his face, he approached the reception desk where a young male in his early twenties was staring at a computer screen, eyes bloodshot and weary. He didn't notice Davies approaching and it took a firm clearing of his throat before the boy looked up.

"Boro na se voithiso? Can I help you?" he said, tired yet helpful.

Where to start?

"I'm here to see Zoe..."

Shit!

The young man smiled patiently, waiting for the surname.

"Never mind. I am a detective working with the Greek police. Has Detective Konsa come through here?"

"Ah. You are English. My English not so good. Detective Konsa is here. He asked for Zoe, also."

"And you sent him to her?"

"Yes. Why I not?"

Fuck. Karagounis couldn't have gotten through.

"Where can I find him?"

"You go through door here." Pointing to a set of double doors to the right of reception. "Go straight. Take stairs up to floor two. It is called Cretian Ward."

Davies was already moving, bursting through the double doors and running down the corridor. A doctor nearly collided with him as he came out of a patient's room, shouting what Davies assumed were obscenities after him.

He took the stairs two at a time, hauling on the black gloss handrail, his shoes squeaking on the highly polished steps. The lights must have been set to a motion detector yet were struggling to keep up with his pace. They flicked on four to six steps too late, leaving Davies to trust his rhythm and the builders' expertise to keep the steps evenly spaced and all the correct height.

Crashing through more double doors, this time painted gloss red, he was on the second floor. On the wall opposite were blue and white signs pointing to various wards and departments. They were in both Greek and English. Third arrow down to the right was the one sign for Cretian Ward. The hall was deserted which only heightened the sounds of his squeaking rubber soled walking boots on the polished floor.

He could hear his heart beating in his ears. The sound of his increasingly heavy breathing surprised him.

Not as fit as you once were, old man.

The corridor ended at a double-glazed window that marked a T-junction. From a few metres out, he could see that the signs below the window directed him to the left if he wanted the Cretian Ward. Half skidding, he took the left and came to sudden stop. Up ahead, maybe five metres, there was a body crumpled on the floor.

Oh shit. I'm too late.

Scanning the area and wishing he had a weapon of some kind; he tentatively approached the prone body. They were wearing hospital scrubs. Another victim in all this mess. Sticking to the right-hand wall, he could see that the door behind the body was emblazoned with Cretian Ward. The body was small, and its back was towards Davies.

He crouched as his approached and whispered "Hello. Are you okay?"

No response.

Keeping one eye on the door, he laid a hand on the person's side. He felt the chest expand gently.

Thank God. Still breathing.

He circled round and found that it was a woman, a large lump on her forehead with a trickle of blood. A stethoscope hung awkwardly from her neck, resting on a name badge. Davies twisted it to read the name. Dr Mekhani. He glanced up at the closed double green doors, staying crouched and below the rectangular glass inserts.

"Sorry, Doctor," he whispered, grabbing here roughly under the arms and dragging her back to the corner he'd last come round. He propped her up against the wall just as she came round. She lashed out at him, struggling.

"Shhh" He hissed "It's ok. I'm a friend. I'm not here to hurt you."

The doctor slowed her struggle, her eyes fighting to focus on him. He backed away, hands in the air in surrender. "My name is Antony Davies. I am a police officer from England. Are you ok? Is Zoe okay?"

"Zoe?" Mekhani said groggily, then suddenly aware, "Zoe!"

"*Is* she okay?" he repeated. "What happened?"

"You must be quick!" she whispered. "It is the detective. Doctor Karagounis phoned me. Warned me. But I couldn't stop him. He was too strong." She tentatively touched the lump on her head and winced.

Still tender.

"Will you be okay?" Davies asked, pleased that Karagounis had made the call, but felt guilty as hell that another innocent had been hurt because of it.

Mekhani nodded and pushed him away "Go! Be careful!"

With one last check that she was okay, he dashed off back towards the Cretian Ward doors and poked his head up to the glass. What he saw shocked him into immediate action.

There were eight beds up against the far wall, three of them empty and one, second from the right, occupied. Here the large and imposing body of Detective Konsa was framed by the moonlit window that sat above the bed. Machines surrounded the hospital bed, one of which was flashing red and even through the door he could hear its warning shriek.

Davies burst through the doors, the sound of which startled the large detective who twisted to see who had come into the ward. In doing so he raised his hands enough so that the small woman in the bed became visible to Davies.

Konsa had been holding a pillow down over Zoe's face, smothering and suffocating her. The movement had allowed her to push the cushion away from her face, and she gasped a large lungful of air.

Hearing her take a breath, Konsa overcame his shock at seeing Davies and twisted back round to resume his attack on the poor girl.

Zoe had regained enough composure and kicked out at her attacker, catching him near his groin. He grunted under the force of the blow.

"Leave her alone!" Davies shouted, urged into action by Zoe's fight. He made short work of the four strides across the room and leapt at the big Greek man, wrapping an arm around his sweaty neck.

Konsa let go of the off-white pillow and grappled at Davies' arm, trying to release the pressure on his airway. Davies was at a disadvantage being four inches shorter than Konsa. He couldn't exact the right pressure on his neck without jumping up and hanging off him like a child who was scared of the spider on the floor.

Konsa backed up, his powerful legs sending both he and Davies backwards until Davies made contact with another unoccupied bed, his lower back taking the full blow from the metal frame, causing him to release pressure on his hold.

Konsa took the advantage and wrenched at Davies' arm, twisting and releasing himself from the hold. He turned to face Davies and growled.

"Fucking English. Always sticking noses into other people's business."

Davies rubbed his back, hoping that it hadn't irritated an old football injury. "When your business is hurting people, *Detective*, it makes it very much my business." He almost spat the word detective, letting Konsa know what he really felt about him.

Konsa laughed, loud and hearty. "You silly man. You are too weak for Konsa. I will fucking kill you both!" To add extra malice to his words, he pulled out a knife from a leather holder tucked under his left arm. Davies hadn't spotted that before, not wanting to get too close to the overweight and pungent man.

The knife was easily four inches long with a fixed black handle. The blade was smooth and sharp on one edge, the fluorescent lights of the ward glinting off it as he twisted the blade, mimicking the twisted grin on his face. The other edge was serrated and looked quite frankly terrifying. Davies didn't fancy getting ripped by that.

Without any bad guy small talk, Konsa lunged at Davies with all the grace of a rhino. Honestly, a partially sighted sloth could have seen the attack coming, and Davies easily darted out of the way, dodging to the right, away from the right-handed lunge of Konsa.

Konsa' momentum took him clattering into the same high footed bed that Davies had crashed into. Davies spun, looking for a weapon of his own, but the surgically clean room offered up very little.

Konsa had regained his footing and growled at Davies, sweat beading on his brow. He pulled at the knotted tie around his neck and loosened it.

Tiring, big man?

Davies stood on his toes, staying nimble, ready to move, watching the blade, never letting his eyes off it.

Concentrate.

Konsa moved, lunged again, his ham-sized fist dwarfing the blade's handle. Davies half twisted and batted Konsa's arm away, making contact with his forearm. Konsa tensed and brought the knife back in towards Davies for another strike, but he easily batted it away again, using the momentum of the attack to get the weapon as far away from him as possible.

Davies stole a glance at the bed where Zoe was awake, sat with her legs tucked up close to her body, chin resting on her knees, her eyes wide with fear. Davies tried to give her a lopsided grin to reassure her, but she only had eyes for the blade.

Good girl.

Konsa swiped at Davies, and he jumped backwards out of the way, but not quick enough. The tip of the blade nicked his torso, easily slicing through his shirt and drawing blood. He grunted in anticipated pain, yet he felt very little, the adrenalin pulsing through his system. He dared not look to see how bad it was, wary of once again losing sight of the lethal blade.

Got to bring this to an end.

Again Konsa lunged.

The distance between them was small and Davies stepped in towards his attacker, jabbing both hands into Konsa's forearm, pushing the bladed arm away.

Konsa tensed, his strength was impressive despite the lack of agility. Davies strained against the one arm of Konsa, pushing hard, down and away.

Konsa's right knee was out in front of him where he'd lunged. Davies took a chance and unbalanced himself to lift his own right leg and kick at Konsa's knee.

The big man howled. All his strength went away from his attack, his knee buckling, and he half collapsed, taking Davies with him.

Need to get that knife off him.

They hit the ground in a crumpled mess, but Davies refused to let go of the forearm that gripped the knife. He scrambled up and dug his knee into Konsa's chest. He started to use his grip on his arm to slam it and the knife onto the linoleum floor. Konsa grunted with every hit but still he held on.

The big man tried to twist up and away to get Davies off him, but in doing so Davies' knee slipped up and onto Konsa's neck. His eyes bulged with the pressure and his grip on the knife faltered enough for the next blow to send it skipping away on the floor and under an empty bed.

Taking advantage of the unexpected slice of fortune, Davies applied more pressure with his knee, taking a worryingly perverse pleasure in the panic in Konsa's eyes. "You bastard!" Davies cursed, spittle flying from his mouth, rage taking over. "You are a Policeman! People trust us!"

Konsa grunted, trying to push Davies away and off him but Davies was pumped and wouldn't relent. "Give up you bastard!" Davies shouted, losing control. "I will fucking end you!"

He felt Konsa begin to weaken, running out of air. The big man began to flail wildly, desperation settling in.

Then, pain. Scorching, scything and blinding pain!

What the hell?!

Looking down he saw where the pain had come from. His shirt was soaked in blood. His blood. Konsa's flailing arm had hit him where the knife had sliced into his flesh.

Konsa took advantage and threw all his weight into hurling Davies off of him. Davies collapsed in a heap, clutching his torso.

Get up man!

Konsa had rolled onto his side, coughing and spluttering, sucking in air, refuelling his starved brain. He recovered first and climbed to his feet, prompting Davies to do the same, grimacing as he did so. The knife was out of reach, leaving both men unarmed.

Konsa lunged at Davies, both arms reaching out. The Greek gripped Davies by the shirt before the Englishman could react. Releasing his right hand, Konsa pulled back and aimed a punch at Davies.

Davies felt the fist connect with his cheek bone, hearing the crack of his eye socket breaking. Blinding, searing pain shot through him but quickly turned numb.

The pair of them had backed up against the wall between two of the beds with Davies' back firmly against the freshly painted white wall. He clamoured to find something, anything to use as a weapon. His hand wrapped around something smooth and heavy.

What's that?

It didn't matter. He gripped it, lifted and swung. He saw a red blur at the end of his arm.

Is that an extinguisher?

The metal tube connected with Konsa's head, knocking him sideways, eyes flying up into his lids, releasing his grip on Davies once more.

He went down to his knees, showing amazing strength to not have been knocked clean out. The big man shook his head to clear the fog.

"You and the bitch have to die!" he roared.

Davies ditched the extinguisher, determined to finish this with his own hands. He swung a right hook down into Konsa's face. Pain lanced up through his hand, but he blocked it out. He swung a left, Konsa unable to react and get out of the way. The fat man's sweaty face helped deflect the blow, but it was still enough to crack his head to one side.

Finish this.

Davies grabbed Konsa's head with both hands and brought his right knee up into the Greeks chin, snapping his head backwards, knocking him out cold. Any harder and he would have killed him.

Konsa's body slumped to the floor. Davies held his fists, waiting for another come back.

He's done.

Davies let out a breath, unaware that he'd been holding it. Stepping over the Greek man, he approached the still cowering Zoe.

"Are you ok?" Davies asked, his head spinning.

Zoe nodded. "Your face…"

Davies tried to grin, but the pain lanced up through his brain and he felt the darkness wash over him, and the world went dark.

Chapter Eleven

Davies awoke, enjoying the darkness. He slowly came to, silently assessing his injuries. It all came back to him, clear as day. The accident. The rush. The fight. He opened his eyes but only one would respond. He reached up to find a thick bandage wrapped around his head, covering an eye that he remembered was probably suffering from a broken socket. Movement caught his good eye, and he swivelled his head on the soft and fluffy pillow.

"Good morning," Karagounis said, smiling warmly, her broken arm in a sling. "How are you feeling?"

"Like I've been hit by a kebab van," he said, trying out his own smile, expecting pain.

Noticing his anxious smile, Karagounis said, "Don't worry. You're hooked up to some morphine. You can smile all you want, although that might make the bone knit awkwardly."

"And make me ugly?"

Karagounis feigned shock. "You think you are handsome?"

Davies didn't argue. He'd never considered himself handsome but had hoped the doctor saw something in him. "Konsa?" He asked

"Arrested and heading for a long time in prison"

"And Zoe?"

"She is recovering well. Talks highly of you!"

Davies smiled awkwardly. "And you?"

"Oh, I'm your last concern?" She said, the gentle sarcasm easy to detect.

"Well, it's hard to be nice to someone who doesn't even share their first name..."

The doctor smiled warmly. "You already know it, Antony."

"I do?" Davies said, worried that the blows to his head had smacked his brain about too much.

"Of course you do. It's Doc!" She laughed heartily at her own terrible joke.

He let it go and just bathed in the warmth of her merriment. They quietly enjoyed each other's company while Doctor Mekhani came by and checked in on them. She was happy with his state and agreed to make sure a cup of coffee was brought down to him. After she left,

Davies wanted to know what had happened. Had they managed to get a confession out of Konsa?

"They have," she said, nodding grimly. "As you know, Joao killed Pippa down at the beach, angered by her supposed relationship with Zoe. They'd had an argument before she began her shift."

"Hence her being ratty at work and the argument with Victor."

"Exactly. He panicked and phoned Konsa."

"Why?"

"Turns out they were old teammates when they played football. Joao had helped Konsa out so he could get a job in the police. Apparently he's... was pretty good with a computer and wiped Konsa's record clean."

"What had he done?"

The Doc screwed up her face. "Amongst other things, attempted rape."

"Fucker."

"Anyway, with his record clean, he joined the police. Since then, he's always owed Joao, and this time, Joao cashed it in. He told him where and how to leave the body and promised to protect him. But then you came along."

"Now he had to change up his game plan. Not so easy to cover it all up when you're not the only one looking into it."

"Exactly."

Davies interrupted. "So the pizza cutter. He saw it alright, but ignored it. Guess he never got round to going back and retrieving it."

"I guess so. Once you cottoned on to Joao, Konsa decided that he needed to clean house and so he was the one who flew that drone into Joao up on the cliffs."

Davies shook his head in frustration, the movement sending a wave of nausea through him. "I should have seen it... wait. What about Zoe? Who was that?"

"That was Konsa. Turns out he had a thing for her, and when she rejected him, he, well, tried to kill her. Figured that, if need be, he could pin that on Joao."

"But didn't want to risk Joao speaking up and revealing his secret. Post death, he could have blamed Zoe's death on Joao, too."

"Could he though?" The doctor asked, confused. "We saw Joao die which means although Konsa could have pinned the attempted murder on Joao, the actual kill, here, would have been after Joao died."

"True," Davies agreed. "But he was smothering her. Leaving no evidence. Once she'd suffocated, we and the doctors would have assumed she'd finally succumbed to the poisoning, no?"

Karagounis grimaced, knowing that to be true. "We'd have seen no reason to suspect anything else and even if I did, Konsa would have blocked any follow up blood work. He would have totally covered his tracks. I imagine you'd still have your suspicions, but I don't see how we could have proven anything."

Davies sighed, resignation written all over his face. "No doubt about it. I couldn't have pinned anything on Konsa. His own ignorance and self-belief undid him. Had Zoe died from his first attempt, he would have gotten away with it. Her determination to live ultimately brought him down."

Karagounis looked genuinely shocked. "I think, DCI Davies, you are downplaying your part in all this. Look at the state of you! You saved the day." She rose up off her chair and placed a hand gently on his arm. "On behalf of the Island of Kos, I thank you."

With that, she leaned in as if she was going to kiss him, but paused and drew back slightly. Davies hadn't realised he was holding his breath, until it came out, full of disappointment, like the depressing deflation of a balloon. In that moment he'd realised that he no longer felt any guilt in his attraction to her. Eleanor had left him behind. Perhaps she had done him a favour. He was willing to take the chance and then this. Rejection? Why? He thought he'd read the situation, seen the signs. But no.

Fool.

Karagounis smiled and hope came back.

"DCI Antony Davies. If you want to know my real name, you better make this a good kiss." Then she leant in again and their lips met, soft and gentle, building into a long passionate kiss.

Breathless, their lips parted and they enjoyed a knowing smile together. "How was that?" He asked.

"Not bad. Seven out of ten." Her smile betraying her true feelings.

"Seven?! Wow. You are hard to impress, Doctor. But is it enough to earn me the honour of knowing you name?"

Unable to keep up the rues, she gave in. "Aella. My name is Aella."

Davies nodded his approval. "From the Greek word meaning Whirlwind. Perfect."

He savoured the look of surprise on her face. "You knew?" she asked.

He just shrugged it off with a smile.

"So, what now?" asked Karagounis, rolling her eyes.

"I tell you what, I could murder a cocktail right about now."

Aella Karagounis smiled. It lit up her face and made Davies' heart bounce. He hadn't felt like this since he was a teenager. "Really?" she purred. "What's your poisin?"

He tried to smile back. "Have you ever tried an espesso martini?"

THE END

Thank you for taking a gamble on this Novella and I hope you enjoyed it! If you did, please be kind enough to leave a review and keep your eyes peeled for the next instalment for DCI Davies!

You can keep up to date with new book launches on my Facebook page:

Scott A A Butler Author.

To follow my personal adventures around the world, check me out at Splitlip Adventures on Facebook, Instagram and You Tube.

Scott Is an author, firefighter and adventurer who lives in North Devon, England with his wife Louise. Keen to fill every spare moment with something productive, writing is one of the few times he actually sits still!

Also from Scott

Reprisal – A Gabriel Quinn Thriller.

First Times and Cupcakes – The story of Scott's attempt to do something new every day for a year.

Chaos and Frog Investigate Series – Childrens picture books featuring the exploits of a dog and cat duo that investigate crimes in their village.

- **The case of the missing fishing nets**
- **The falling lights**

Dipping Toes in Literary waters – Volume One and Two.

Printed in Great Britain
by Amazon